Arabian Noir

Quadrant Books

Published in 2024 by Quadrant Books

A member of the Memoirs Group
Suite 2, Top Floor, 7 Dyer Street, Cirencester, Gloucestershire, GL7 2PF

Copyright ©Michael Lynes and Alex Shaw
Michael Lynes and Alex Shaw have asserted their rights under the Copyright Designs and Patents Act 1988 to be identified as the authors of this work.

The moral rights of the authors has been asserted by them in accordance with the Copyright, Designs and Patents Act, 1988

All rights reserved.
No part of this publication may be reproduced, stored in a retrieval system, or transmitted in any form or by any means, without the prior permission in writing of the publisher, nor be otherwise circulated in any form of binding or cover other than that in which it is published and without a similar condition including this condition being imposed on the subsequent purchaser

Reasonable efforts have been made to find the copyright holders of any third party copyright material. An appropriate acknowledgement can be inserted by the publisher in any subsequent printing or edition

A catalogue record for this book is available from the British Library

Arabian Noir
Paperback ISBN 978-1-7384598-0-3

Printed and bound in Great Britain

Arabian noir

Short stories curated by the Gulf Chapter of the
CRIME WRITERS' ASSOCIATION

Contents

Foreword
A note from the editors
Murder in the Middle East - a Poem by Paul A. Freeman

The Reddest Dress - Sara Hamdan 1
The Cost of Air - Moxie T. Anderson 15
The Gardener - Michael Lynes 37
Dubai Heat - Alex Shaw 48
The Writers - Annabel Kantaria 79
Say My Name - Gal Podjarny 92
Round peg in a square hole - Padmini Sankar 103
Solid Evidence - Paul A. Freeman 120
Miss Pleasance Goes East - Daisy Line 129
Crescents are Perfect - Rohini Sunderam 148
The Thing About Maryam - Mohanalakshmi Rajakumar 164
Footnote - Glen R Stansfield 174
Jack and the Box - by S.G. Parker 192

Foreword

✕

In a 2014 article by blogger Marcia Lynx Qualey, entitled 'The Mysterious Fall and Rise of the Arab Crime Novel,' Qualey examined the early infatuation by Arabian readers – especially Egyptians – of western crime fiction, in particular the novels of Maurice Leblanc featuring gentlemen-thief Arsene Lupin. According to Qualey, Lupin became "one of the most famous popular fiction figures in the 20th century Egyptian literary imagination." (The first Arabic translation of a Lupin adventure was published in 1910).

But Qualey also tells us that: "Detective fiction has had a long relationship with Arab readers." She reminds us of a story that first made an appearance in *One Thousand and One Nights,* the collection of (folk) tales told by Scheherazade to her new husband and liege lord Shahryār to forestall her execution. One might say that Scheherazade, by stopping each night at a critical juncture in the tale – thus forcing the king to wait another impatient night for the conclusion – practically invented the cliffhanger that is now *de rigueur* in modern thrillers.

The tale – *The Three Apples* – is gruesome in a way modern crime readers would, no doubt, appreciate. A fisherman "discovers a locked chest near the Tigris River and sells it to the caliph, Harun al-Rashid. Inside, the Abbasid ruler finds the body of a young woman hacked to pieces and orders his vizier to solve the crime in three days. If he fails, the vizier will be executed." Thankfully for the protagonists of contemporary crime novels, the threat of being put to death in event of failure is no longer a consideration – one suspects Hercule Poirot might react less than favourably to such a Damoclean situation as he fires up his little grey cells.

The Three Apples also features one of the earliest twist endings in literature, when the vizier discovers that the ultimate culprit – whose theft of an apple led to the murder of our victim (by a husband who wrongly assumed his wife had been unfaithful) is none other than his own slave. We can, with our modern sensibilities, pass judgment on the issues raised in the story – murder as punishment for infidelity, slaveholding – but we must also acknowledge that this potent tale encapsulates many of the devices and tropes that we now take for granted in crime fiction.

The *Arabian Noir* anthology represents a milestone for the Crime Writers Association's (CWA) Gulf Chapter. Editor-authors Michael Lynes and Alex Shaw have compiled a collection that foregrounds tales of murder and mystery either set in the locality or linked to it via authors' connections to the region. The diversity of the collection is a testament to the widespread enthusiasm for the genre around the Gulf region, and the ability of literature to act as a means of bringing people together, at a time when, one suspects, the region most needs it.

Showcasing a wide range of styles, the author contributors have employed the short story form to present readers with insights into human frailty, new vistas, and intellectual challenges to bamboozle the most ardent Christie enthusiast. The collection proves, once again, that there is room in the crime fiction stable for all manner of writers ... and readers! With this in mind, the CWA's Gulf Chapter aims to promote crime writing in all its guises across the region.

My own love affair with the Gulf began a long time ago. Although born and raised in England, in my twenties I spent a decade in India as a management consultant. During that time, my company undertook a side project in Kuwait, an eye-opening introduction to the Gulf states. I discovered that fuel was cheaper than drinking water, and that the Arab world was richer in history and local stories than I could possibly have imagined.

Years later, after I was first published, I was invited to speak at the Emirates Festival of Literature in Dubai where, for reasons that, at first, mystified me, I was placed on a panel with British TV gardening celebrity, Alan Titchmarsh. (It later turned out that the incredibly personable Titchmarsh wrote fiction – though not crime fiction.) My recollections of that trip? An incredibly well organised festival, the glitz and glamour of downtown Dubai, and a trip out to the desert to ride a very surly camel, before enjoying a night under the stars in a Bedouin tent in the company of some of the most famous writers on the planet.

Crime fiction has taken me around the world, allowing me to meet people I would never otherwise have been able to. It has been a long journey. It took me over two decades – and seven rejected novels – to find an agent. My debut was eventually published in 2015. *The Unexpected Inheritance of Inspector Chopra* is about a middle-aged policeman in Mumbai, India who solves murders, whilst having to deal with the somewhat unusual problem of inheriting a one-year-old baby elephant. The book went on to become a bestseller and was published in 17 languages, in effect, giving me a career. But the book did something else. It proved to British publishers that crime fiction audiences have an appetite for stories set beyond the traditional English village (where, apparently, you can murder half the population without anyone so much as batting an eyelid) or the gritty streets of London or Edinburgh or New York or Los Angeles.

Currently, I write historical crime novels, the Malabar House series, featuring India's first female police detective, paired with an English forensic scientist working in Bombay. The books are set in 1950s India, just a few years after Independence, Gandhi's assassination, and the horrors of Partition. They are mysteries written in a Golden Age style: cryptic clues and red herrings abound. More importantly, the books embrace a strong sense of place, and period, and allow me to explore issues such as post-colonialism, and the place of women in Indian society. Crime fiction's strength is its ability to dissect social issues whilst entertaining. And in the Arabian Noir collection we see this dynamic played out with flair and insight.

In 2023, I was elected as the first non-white Chair of the 70-year-old Crime Writers Association, the largest and oldest association of crime writers in Europe. It goes without saying that chairing the CWA is an honour. More importantly, my appointment sends a signal. Namely, that the crime genre is inclusive *and* representative of the true tastes of readers. Crime fiction has led the way in opening itself up to new voices and new stories. And why not? As I often joke, criminals are the most diversity conscious members of our society – they will happily murder, rob, loot, or kidnap anyone regardless of creed, colour, or background.

I write a lot of short stories. It's a genre I am particularly fond of. The secret to a great short story? Start fast, ride hard, and finish with a kick. Collections such as Arabian Noir are important in maintaining the tradition of the noir short story, whilst moving the boundaries so that a more diverse range of tales can fit under the short fiction umbrella. Crime is the world's most popular genre for a reason, and short stories play an important role in spreading the gospel. After all, who doesn't love a good murder?

Finally, a few thank yous. To publisher, Quadrant Books, for generously supporting this work. To editors Michael and Alex, for their tireless championing of crime fiction in the region. To the authors who have contributed their dark and deadly offerings. And, last but never least, to the readers who will, hopefully, embrace this collection.

Warm regards,

Vaseem Khan
Chair, Crime Writers' Association

A note from the editors

This anthology started life in late 2022 over a cup of coffee in Dubai. It was Alex's idea, as is the title, *Arabian Noir*. It was our first meeting as the only two members of the newly formed Gulf Chapter of the CWA. We wanted to do something to promote writing in the region, and in particular crime writing. As Vaseem Khan, the Chair of the CWA says:

"The CWA is a home for all crime writers, whether you've sold 10m copies or 10. It should be a place where writers of all backgrounds can come and know they will be treated with respect. Ultimately, the CWA should be about inspiring the next generation of crime writers."

We'd like to thank our growing gang of crime writers in the region for their support. In particular, Annabel Kantaria, who has been an invaluable source of advice and encouragement.

This is the first anthology created by a chapter in the CWA's seventy-year history, and we hope you enjoy reading these stories as much as we did. Who knows, you may be reading, 'Number 1,' in a long running series of CWA Gulf Chapter anthologies. There are certainly enough crime stories about vengeance, justice, redemption and hope to feed the imagination of authors and keep our readers entertained.

Michael Lynes and Alex Shaw
Dubai, January 2024

Murder in the Middle East

by Paul A. Freeman

Amidst the sand and shifting dunes lurks Death!

A hookah pipe is wrapped around a neck,

and tightened till it wrings a final breath.

Then on an Arab dhow's pearl-laden deck

a long, curved blade, beneath a crescent moon,

is flashing as it finds a victim's heart.

And in a harem, see a maiden swoon -

that dish of poisoned dates has played its part.

Or in a picturesque oasis, drowned,

a body in a shroud-like dish-dash floats.

While mummified, an ancient corpse is found

amongst the desert bushes grazed by goats.

Upon our tales of crime and murder, feast,

and read about a darker Middle East.

The Reddest Dress

by Sara Hamdan

••••

I eye the gold clock on the wall. I've been on my feet for at least four straight hours, my arms moving rhythmically back and forth blow-drying women's hair. The lady currently in the chair scrolls endlessly on her phone. The glint of her diamond ring is razor sharp.

"Ouch! Careful," she says, raising her eyebrow at me in the mirror. She puts a hand to her hair, half silky smooth, half wet and untamed.

New salon is so-so, hairdresser nearly burned my scalp right off, she types to a friend. *Think I'll wear my new Dior tonight. See you at Roberto's at 8?*

I smile an apology when she catches me reading her text. I check the clock again. When I finish, there is no tip, and I am not surprised. It does, however, mean I have to take the bus home. Again.

I watch the ebb and flow of headlights as I wait for the bus. I stand in the darkness beneath the sign. I have survived three summers in Dubai, yet the daily slap of heat is always a surprise. Sweat pools in every dark little corner of my body. I wipe the wetness above my lip with a crumpled tissue from my purse. The strap is about to break.

I wonder what people in their air-conditioned cars, with leather seats and pleasant music, must think when they look at me? Do they even notice me, standing in the dark in my plain black dress and my polite black ballet flats, with my inoffensive bun?

The bus slows in front of me, making the whining noises of a yawning old dog. The doors swing open, and I walk up the steps. I swipe my card. I sit.

On the highway, we hurtle past a row of skyscrapers, standing tall like rows of giant lipsticks. We leave the main city and its elegant lights behind. The dance of people coming on and off the bus keeps going until we reach my neighborhood, with low-rise buildings the color of sand. Colorful laundry hangs on balconies and neon light displays scream from shopfronts on the ground floor. A strong scent of curry accompanies me on my short walk to my block.

I arrived at my apartment building in Satwa. I greet the friendly Ethiopian woman who sells baked goods from a plastic bag on the corner. She offers me fragrant coffee in a plastic cup. I shouldn't drink it because it keeps me up at night, but I accept it. The warmth in my hand feels good as I step into the cool lobby of my building. The blonde flight attendant who lives on the third floor holds the elevator door open for me.

"Long day?" she asks. Her uniform is creased.

Not at all, I want to say. *I got my hair done and I'm going to wear the Dior tonight. Want to join us at Roberto's at 8?*

"Yeah, can't wait for a cold shower and an early night," I say. "This heat is just…"

"Unbreath-able," she answers, her Slavic accent strong. "Is that a right word in English? Like, hard to breathe?"

I nod as she gets off on her floor.

I sip the cardamom-infused coffee. I let my hair down. Fifth floor. I can smell onion and garlic in the corridor as I put my key in the lock. Elisabetta must be home.

"Ciao, *cara*," she says. She is busy at the stove, wearing a fluffy bathrobe with a towel on her head. "I don't want to smell like the food, so I cover my hair. I see Amir later. Hungry?"

I nod, tossing the empty coffee cup in the bin.

She walks up to me with a wooden spoon dripping with herby tomato sauce. It tastes like a romantic comedy. No wonder she has a lover, and I am still single.

"Please teach me how to cook," I beg. I put my purse down on the small counter. "Is Amir coming by here? I can stay in my room so you can enjoy a movie night."

"No, no, we go out," she laughs. "He will take me to a nice, new hotel his friend is opening on the Palm. Fancy. But food they pass around trays is so tiny at these events, I don't understand these people. I need to eat a real dinner first."

She piles two plates with ribbons of pasta, telling me about her boss's latest tantrum at work. We call him The Child. She has to be nice to The Child because he is her boss, but also because he technically introduced her to Amir. Amir was coming in for a wealth management consultation when he laid eyes on Elisabetta's smile behind the bank's sleek reception desk. He quickly became a client - and much more - after that day three months ago.

We finish and I wash the dishes. She grabs my hand and leads me to her bedroom. Elisabetta is very neat. Her sparse room has powder pink walls and a white desk featuring makeup essentials in small boxes. The shaggy rug is soft under my worn feet. I sit on her bed.

"I have to show you what he buy me, crazy man," she says.

She opens a box and lifts out a cream-colored Chanel purse. I hold it carefully with both hands, half expecting it to purr as I stroke it.

"Just gorgeous, he has really elegant taste, honestly," I gush at the buttery leather. "I'm happy he treats you so well. Gives me hope."

She smiles at me as she slips into a structured navy dress with subtle side cutouts. I haven't seen her wear it before. Must be another one of Amir's gifts.

She places the purse back into its box, then does a drum roll on its surface.

"Okay, I save best for last to show you," she says.

She crosses to the bedroom door and closes it. Hanging on a hook behind the door is a white garment bag with the words Elie Saab on it in simple black font. She unzips it and I can see bright red inside, the color seeping out as if she were slowly slicing open a white animal.

"I know!" she squeals.

Holding it up to catch the light, the dress is a medley of small beads, feathers and layered fabric that falls in waves. It is every shade of red, all in one dress.

"Is this what love at first sight feels like?" I sigh, running my fingers over it. She hangs the dress back up on the hook and we both sit on the bed, staring at it in revered silence.

After a minute or so, I feel Elisabetta moving around me. She gets up to check her phone, blot lipstick, make small talk. I nod and smile at the right parts. My eyes keep finding their way back to the dress, the way it seems to come alive in the light when I tilt my head slightly. I wonder how it would melt onto a human body. My body?

Amir is downstairs in an idling car. Elisabetta gives me a kiss on the cheek and reminds me that we have run out of coffee. She waves me off and I hear the front door slam.

I am alone, sitting on my roommate's bed, a long night of quiet stretching before me.

I should soak my feet and watch reality TV. I could answer my mum's call, listen to her veiled comments about her neighbor in Devon who has a dutiful daughter who visits her regularly, her GP whose daughter is getting married, her vicar whose niece has learned how to bake the perfect summer tart. Dubai doesn't have seasons; she likes to remind me. Or men who commit. We would then argue about the weather.

I stand. I mean to leave Elisabetta's room, but instead, I shut the door and let my eyes drink in the redness of this decadent dress. A zing of excitement greets my fingertips when I caress it again.

Where would I even wear a dress like this? I think back to the last time I had fun, real fun, laughter-from-the-deepest-depths-of-my-core kind of fun, and... I have to think harder.

So I stop thinking. I take my work clothes off, leaving them in a black pile in Elisabetta's spotless room. I carefully remove the delicate straps of the dress off the hanger. It is on my body like second skin within seconds. It brushes my knees as I move. I walk three steps to the mirror, zipping myself up easily in the back. The red dress brings out honey tones in my hair and eyes. With my hands, I pile my dark hair up on my head, with loose tendrils falling all over my face. I use a spider-shaped hair claw on Elisabetta's vanity desk to keep it in place. I grab red lipstick, the lucky one that she wore the day she met Amir. I put it on.

Mascara wand in hand, I feel like my own fairy godmother. I stare at myself in the mirror with fresh eyes.

I feel the most beautiful I have ever felt in the reddest dress I have ever seen. I smile in a way I never have before. I can't stay in the apartment now. I am restless. I need today to be more than the day that I worked in a salon on my feet for hours on end. But do I dare wear Elisabetta's dress before she has had a chance? Where do I even go, decked out like it's New Year's Eve in the 1920's?

Roberto's at 8, the dress whispers to me.

I tidy the mascara and lipstick back in the makeup box. I notice two hundred Dirham bills on the vanity desk. Elisabetta sets money aside each month for her makeup and fashion purchases. She says she has to keep up with Amir's events, because she wants to feel beautiful, but also because other women are competitive. Would she notice if I borrowed this, too, tonight?

Roberto's at 8, singsongs the dress.

The dress seems to bend time. I don't know how long I stared at it and how long it took me to dress and take the money. After blurry minutes, an Uber arrives to whisk me off to the trendy restaurant. I haven't spent money like this in… I need to think. Harder. A giggle escapes from my lips. I sink into the leather seat, asking the driver to adjust the AC and raise the volume on a song on the radio I don't even know, just because I can. I realize I've left my apartment with only my phone and a small wad of cash tucked into my purse with the flimsy strap.

Maybe I should have borrowed the new Chanel. Too much?

I feel as open as the highway. My heart drums with excitement as we near the city lights. Back in the UK, this is the life people imagine I have in Dubai every day. Flashy, full of nice dinners out, yacht parties and fancy dresses. I don't speak of the daily toil, but tonight, I will have a fun story to tell.

We near the financial district. The car slows to a crawl near the main glass building. The weather is cooler now. I step out of the car, the clack of my high heels mixing with the laughter that rises from the bars and restaurants around me. I pass the bus stop where I stood mere hours before, after my shift. Roberto's is near my salon, but I take the long way to avoid seeing my place of work. I am a different woman tonight.

There is a queue outside Roberto's, where a large man in a black shirt stands in front of a velvet rope. I wonder if this happens every night or if there is someone famous inside.

"Is your name on the list?" I hear the woman holding a clipboard asking the first person in the queue. I feel a flutter of nerves. Why did I think I belonged here? My heart pounds against my ribcage and I put my hands behind my back, hiding my cheap bag with the flimsy strap.

"Miss? Excuse me, Woman in Red?" says the woman with the clipboard.

I look up. Our eyes lock. What did I do?

She motions for me to come towards her.

"Saw that dress on Gigi Hadid on the runway yesterday. To die for. Please, go right ahead," she motions to the man in black to let me in.

I am in! I am seen! I am special!

The dress is in charge tonight.

I can't find my voice, so I just give a small smile like this is my normal life. I walk in, heady music growing louder. An olive tree lit with fairy lights sits at the center of the dim restaurant. Crowds of people stand at the bar, moving to the music and lighting cigarettes. Diners chat at tables with multiple forks and spoons at each setting. A woman cuts into a piece of red meat and smiles when she catches my eye.

I put my shoulders back and walk slowly, wading into the scene. A man takes my hand and twirls me around. I laugh. Another hands me a drink. I position myself by the bar. I listen to snippets of conversations flutter around me about foreign exchange rates, summer holidays in French chateaux, equestrian lessons, a new exhibit at Sotheby's.

"Waiting for someone?" asks a man with bright blue eyes. He has a soft accent. Maybe German?

"Yes, a friend, though running fashionably late," I lie. The lies seem to come easily tonight.

"I'm here with colleagues, but I've seen enough of them today. Could I entertain you a little instead?" he asks, offering to refresh my drink. I nod. A woman appears by his side.

"Ah, Rania, one my colleagues," says The German by way of introduction. "Rania, this is..."

I look into the eyes of the woman who sat in my salon chair earlier today. I am happy to see she has recovered from the terrible trauma of me tugging slightly too hard while I blow-dried her hair.

Standing face to face, she looks smaller than I remember. Her scowl is the same.

"Rose," I lie, extending my hand. "Your hair looks lovely."

Rania eyes me a little closely, but I know she will not recognize me. How could she, when she barely looked at me properly during the hour we spent together?

"Thank you, I love your dress," she says. "It's exquisite. Your husband must do quite well for himself."

I should feel insulted, but instead I glow in the backhanded compliment. She thinks I am beautiful and wants to know if The German has a shot with me. I look like I fit in here. Tonight, I am Rose. I am wearing an expensive dress, and I could be a trophy wife.

"Rania!" The German says. He shakes his head slightly at me. We have an inside joke already. I know that when Rania leaves us alone, we will talk about crazy colleagues. I can tell him about The Child at Elisabetta's bank.

"No, really, Jakob, you don't know fashion like us ladies do," says Rania, pulling out her phone.

She Googles a picture of my red dress. Gigi Hadid is wearing it. In small font at the bottom of the image, I see that the cost is equal to about one year's rent for me. I remove my elbow from the bar table that has grown sticky. I keep my face still.

I consider another lie. I could tell them I am an heiress here to consider buying Roberto's. Before I can speak, they have changed the conversation to vacations.

"You should come," Jakob turns to me. "Be spontaneous. Get away from this heat. Chamonix or Verbier? Have you ever been off season? No skiing, but the freshest air. We're booking tonight. Last minute trip for the long weekend."

Two more of their friends join our little group. They use phrases I would normally find ridiculous on the reality shows I love to watch. Chalet, business class, Moncler Grenoble, fondue.

These people here, bathed in soft light and upbeat music and beautiful fabrics, they are on show as much as I am. I am jealous of the decisions they make, of the beauty and levity in their world.

How must it feel to fall asleep wondering about your favorite type of champagne, instead of wishing you could afford to call in sick even one single day?

I want it so badly, the ability to easily book an impromptu holiday to an Alpine chalet, the cold stinging my cheeks until they are pink and raw. I think of myself at the bus stop, the humidity crushing my lungs.

"What do you say, Rose?" Jakob teases. "Have we tempted you?"

I shift in my seat. As I edge off the chair, one of the delicate feathers on my dress gets stuck. I move to detach it and, instead, it rips a long seam completely off the body of the dress. In panic, my elbow hits a glass on the bar, spilling a dark, tangy liquid on the other side.

The music and laughter around me continues but, for a moment, everything is perfectly still inside me. I cannot bring myself to look into Rania's eyes and see her smirk. Jakob reaches out a hand to assist me, offering napkins. I take them, grab my purse and keep my head down.

"It barely shows," Jakob reassures me.

"Check it in the bathroom light," Rania suggests.

"I will do that, and when I'm back, maybe I will book that holiday," I say, my voice airier than I feel. "You only live once, right?"

A small cheer erupts from the group as I walk away from the bar. Instead of asking directions to the bathroom, I walk straight out the front door. I place the strap of my purse over my shoulder, and it snaps, spilling the meager contents in front of the queuing people. Money, phone, keys. I gather them with one hand and am already on the move again. I ignore the woman with the clipboard asking why I am leaving so soon.

How will I tell Elisabetta I ruined her dress? How can I possibly repay her? Why did I even show up at Roberto's at 8 tonight? What was I trying to prove to myself? Was this a cruel exercise to see how the other half lives, with their chalets and handsome colleagues?

I keep marching until I find myself in front of the hair salon where I work. In the reflected glass, I look like a red ghost.

The storefront is dark. I cup my hands to better see the stark, white reception desk. The salon has only been in operation for three weeks. Security cameras haven't been installed yet; the security team will arrive on Monday.

And I have the key in my purse.

It's something more than caviar dreams that makes me unlock the door and walk to the safe beneath the cash register. It's a primal urge to live differently. Every cell in my body is fighting the slow death of a slow life. The red dress stoked a fire that has changed me.

I use the napkins Jakob handed me to enter the passcode I have seen Sally-Anne, the store owner, use. Sally-Anne, the kind woman who was in the church choir with my mother. Sally-Anne, who gave me a job when I wanted to live in Dubai.

I touch the safe. It is meant for petty cash and monthly payments of bills. I open it, hoping for just enough money for a good tailor to fix the dress. I move quickly, quietly, like a fox, as if I have done this many times before. The nerves only wash over me when I open the safe to find a stack of money large enough to cover an excellent tailor, perhaps a new dress entirely.

Or even the holiday of a lifetime.

I could do it. I could just leave in the morning and never come back. I could reinvent myself in Verbier. Find a new job, a different way to live. Send Sally-Anne the money eventually. Buy Elisabetta a new dress. Breathe. Really breathe.

My hand is on the stack when the lights come on. I am crouched like an animal, a wild look in my eye. The gentleness in the voices of the two policemen finally breaks my spell.

It was a silent alarm. I wasn't thinking clearly. It was the coffee. The dress. And pure desire. I just wanted something different. Now, I sit in the ruined red dress, wondering where I will be, come morning. The bus stop, the airport or a prison cell?

Elisabetta arrives.

"Sally-Anne didn't press charges. Nobody believes I would be stupid enough to walk in and steal the money outright, using my own key," I tell her. "She confirmed I am a trusted employee. And the policemen were so kind to me."

"You're very lucky. The Child would have jailed me for life," she says. "Nice dress, by the way."

"Now you see what I did to it. I am so sorry, Elisabetta," my voice breaks. "I don't know what's come over me."

She holds my gaze. If she cries, I will burst into tears. She holds my hand, and we lean back on the bench together. I am waiting for a policeman to return my things so we can go home.

"It's fake, *cara*," she whispers.

"What?"

"It's a fake dress. I bought it from this Chinese lady to impress Amir's idiot friends," she says. "I wish you talk to me."

I am processing. I don't know whether to cry or laugh.

"You left your party because I ruined your fake dress and called you from a police station," I said numbly.

We laugh. I am filled with fear at what I have done, what could still happen if Sally-Anne changes her mind.

"I left the party because... my relationship is a little fake, too," she says, closing her eyes. "Amir was there. With his wife."

All this pretense, all around us, has come crashing down in the harsh lights of the clinical police station. We speak in low tones, punctuating stretches of silence with words of comfort and incredulity, before finding ourselves on the street.

We stand at a bus stop. It is nearly 3 am and much cooler than the daytime. We marvel at the safety of our city. We are two women in eye-catching dresses, standing at a bus stop in the dead of night, completely at ease.

"You know what is better than my pasta?" she asks me.

"Your leftover pasta," I smile.

It's the first real smile to spread over my face over the last 24 hours.

The red dress is fake and ruined. But this friendship – at least this is real.

AUTHOR BIOGRAPHY

Sara Hamdan is the global managing editor of Protocol Labs, an American tech VC. After winning a Netflix short story award, she received the Emirates Literature Foundation Seddiqi First Chapter Writers' Fellowship for her debut novel, *What Will People Think?* featuring an Arab American, female stand-up comedian. Sara's novel went on to win a landmark two book deal with Holt and will come out early 2025. A Berkeley and Columbia graduate, Sara has called

Arabian Noir

Dubai home for nearly 20 years. When she's not typing away at her laptop, she loves to spend time at the beach with her husband and two kids.

The Cost of Air

by Moxie T. Anderson

••••

Because the city had a cold snap over the weekend, with icy winds and rain keeping most of the city's residents indoors, the blowflies took longer than usual to begin colonizing the five corpses in the run-down apartment in the eastern area, Old Amman.

Strewn throughout the small apartment, the bodies would remain there for another three days before Inas's older sister Munira threatened to call the police if the landlord did not let her enter. Marwan El Sherbini – a scowling and forever petulant man whose chain smoking lent more age to his face than his years did – argued with Munira for nearly an hour before relenting.

"Haga," Marwan hissed. *Old woman.*

At thirty-four and eight months pregnant, Munira felt the insult like a slap striking her face. She was shivering, pale and haggard; climbing the stairs to Inas's apartment had her wheezing in the cold January winds. "You dare call *me* old?" she snapped, catching her breath. "You, *Abu reiha,* who looks like death is clinging to your dirty old trousers?"

The landlord scowled. "How do I know your sister would want

you in here? I will open the door, but you stay next to me and touch nothing. *Wallah*, I don't need this trouble."

Munira recoiled from his breath, which was a sour blend of cigarettes, coffee, and garlic. "Just open the door. I won't touch anything." The landlord pulled a hefty keyring from his pockets, jingling it around until he finally found the key to the apartment Inas shared with her four children.

In the years following this day, Munira would recall the moment the landlord opened the door countless times, swearing she saw a jinn – a *kafir* demon – crawl from the house in the form of a lizard with tiny spikes protruding from its hide. Of course, a lizard scuttling about in the cold of winter was unlikely, but no one questioned Munira given what she found upon entering the apartment.

What the residents of Old Amman did remember about that cold morning was the howls of agony that echoed through the stone building and the streets when Munira discovered the bodies.

Detective Abdul Farayeh gulped down a thick, almost black Turkish coffee before opening the door to his sedan to step into the street near the crime scene. He shivered and pulled his jacket around himself, but the move was futile in the biting winds.

A new father, Farayeh had slept in the morning hours before his cell phone buzzed, with his captain directing him to the morbid scene in the older area of town. Exhausted, he found himself regretting he hadn't purchased two shots of the strong coffee at the roadside stand along his route into the city proper.

His partner of four years, Zaid Mansour, gingerly shut the door and tried to shield his lighter from the wind so he could light a cigarette. Mansour surveyed the street and grimaced against the icy spatters hitting his face. "I'll have the officers move the bystanders across the street," he said, nodding to the small group gathered in front of the building. "What business do they think they have here?"

"At least it's cold," Farayeh said. "If it wasn't, we'd have twice as many of the *Hamir* to deal with. See you inside."

Farayeh crossed the block and climbed the stairwell in the shabby building, following the sounds of commotion up three flights until he reached a visibly pregnant woman seated on the top step. She was sobbing loudly. An older man huddled in the corner of the stairwell, scowling at his cell phone.

"Ah, detective," a female patrol officer said as Farayeh rounded the landing to the corridor. "We have secured the scene. I should warn you –"

"*Shukran*," the detective said, cutting off the warning. "And these two?" He gestured at the man and woman over his shoulder.

"The victim's sister. The Egyptian is the landlord. They discovered the bodies."

Farayeh slipped on gloves and shoe covers as he listened. "I see. Can you put in a call to have them taken downtown? Make sure the woman is comfortable." He turned back to Munira, whose face was pale with horror and sat next to her. "*Yech'ti*," he said gently. Sister. "I am very sorry for your loss. I'm going to ask an officer to escort you downtown. They will take care of you until I get there. Be strong for your child."

Munira nodded. "You have to catch him," she said, her voice fraught with pain. "This *sharmout* – he killed them all, even the baby!" She began to wail anew, her cries reverberating down the stairwell.

Farayeh motioned for the officer, who bent down to help Munira. "I will catch whoever is responsible," Farayeh said. "Please, go and get some food and tea. I will meet with you as soon as I am finished here. You there –" He raised his voice at the landlord. "You need to go as well."

"How long will this take?" Marwan groused. "I have a lot to do today."

"It will take as long as I need," the detective snapped. "No more, no less. And unless you are an emergency doctor, I think your plans can wait."

Defeated, the landlord swallowed his protests and followed Munira down the steps slowly.

Farayeh turned his attention back to the apartment, where the lab technicians stepped aside as he entered the doorway. Their faces mirrored the three the detective met in the stairwell: peaked from the nightmare within the small apartment.

Although the building was on the verge of being a slum, the apartment itself was well-kept, nearly spotless. Farayeh found himself concerned that the killer or killers may have scoured it and made a note in his notebook before turning his attention to one of the crime scene technicians. "Well?"

"Five deceased, all in the two bedrooms. One adult female, four children ranging in age from about ten to infant. No obvious sign of trauma. *Elhagni.*"

The detective did as he was bid and followed the technician down a tiny hallway past the kitchen, where plates were still stacked in the sink – the one element of mess he observed in the tidy apartment so far. He took down another note in his book.

Arabian Noir

By the time he reached the first bedroom door, Farayeh could smell the distinctive odour of death. The technician stepped into the room, and the detective followed.

The bedroom was tiny and clean, but cold. Two single beds formed a half-square along the edge of the northern wall, and in each bed was the pitiful sight of a young boy, each no older than ten but no younger than six. Their eyes were closed, as if they had shut out the dread of their own deaths. Had it not been for the circumstances and odour, an onlooker might think they were simply deep in slumber.

"Akh," Farayeh said and let out a low whistle. "And the others?"

"This way," the technician said. The pair passed a small bathroom before stepping through the threshold of the second bedroom, where an even more pitiable sight met Farayeh's eyes. A young mother lay between two smaller children, one a rosy-cheeked toddler with soft black curls who was tucked into his mother's left side. On the opposite side, an infant lay between Inas and the wall, a measure she had likely taken to prevent the babe from falling off the bed.

With his newborn safely home with his wife, Farayeh couldn't help but be momentarily queasy, as if someone reached under his rib cage to squeeze his heart. He stepped backward, closed his eyes, and tried to picture his wife at home, safely cradling his daughter.

In taking the step back, he stumbled into the crime scene technician, a serious, bespectacled smaller man who threw up his hands defensively. "Sir?"

"*Bismillah*," Farayeh muttered under his breath. "*La hawla wa la quwwata illa billah.*" *There is no might and no power except for Allah.*

"The forensics photographer has already documented the scene with photographs and video. I think he's outside catching his breath," the technician said. "It is a terrible sight indeed."

The technician stepped away quietly as Farayeh approached the bodies. No blood. He pulled down the collar of Inas's nightshirt but found no obvious signs of strangulation. Her hair was braided, so he pushed a gloved finger into one of the plaits to see if it were still wet, which would be a clue to death by drowning. There was no telltale sign of froth at her mouth or nostrils, though, and her clothes were dry.

As he was assessing the scene, Farayeh heard a sharp intake of breath over his shoulder. He turned around to find his partner, eyes wide, looking at the grim scene. "Strangled?" he asked.

"I'm not sure," Farayeh said. "I saw no signs of strangulation on the mother. I'm praying for the strength to look at the babies."

"And two more in the other room?"

"Yes, I'm afraid so." The men exchanged a pained look. They had worked several murders together in the past few years, but nothing this horrific. Most of the cases they took were crimes of passion and anger; none of the cases had involved children.

Mansour pulled a notebook from his suit pocket and began to jot down notes. His ability to remain professional steeled Farayeh, and he was grateful for his partner's presence. Mansour bent over the sad trio and pulled up the sleeves of the mother's nightshirt and the children's pyjamas. Once again, there were no telling marks. No blood, no obvious trauma.

"Let me show you the other victims," Farayeh said. The pair walked the short distance down the hall to where the boys lay. Mansour examined the bodies here, too, but found no visible signs pointing to the cause of their deaths.

"We will need to get a toxicology report," Mansour said, his dark brows furrowing his forehead. "Maybe she poisoned them and then herself?"

"Definitely a possibility," Farayeh said. "Single mother with all these mouths to feed. Desperation is a tragic bedfellow. I'll have them transport the bodies now."

"And then?"

"Then we speak to the two that found her – a sister and the landlord. They're already on their way to the station."

When the detectives reached the station, they warmed up with another cup of coffee while plotting out their interviews.

"Let's talk to the sister first," Farayeh said. "She needs to go home and find some comfort with her own family. No doubt there will be problems between her family and the estranged husband on the burials."

Mansour looked at his partner, his jaw clenched. "Not if he is responsible for their murders."

The men entered interview room two to find Munira slumped over the table, her head down in her arms. She looked up from the table at the sound of the door opening while keeping her head cradled in her arms. Her tears had dried up, her eyes red and puffy. Her whole demeanour was one of grief and exhaustion.

"*As-Salam*, sister," Fayareh said. He took a seat across from her, Mansour settling in on the folding chair next to him. "I see you have water. Have you had anything to eat?

"I'm not hungry," she said.

"Come, *habibti*," Mansour said soothingly. "Let me get something for you. At least some warm tea."

"*Na'am*," Munira said. "It is so cold in here."

Farayeh hopped up and left the room momentarily, coming back with a warm tea and a heavy gray wool coat about four sizes too large for the grieving woman. He set down the tea and wrapped the jacket around Munira's shoulders. The coat enveloped her tiny frame, making her look as if she were huddled in an entrance to a dark cave.

"*Shukran*," she said softly and took a sip of the tea. "One of the officers said she would call my husband."

"We will check on that for you, yes," Farayeh assured her. "I certainly don't want you to drive home alone after – this morning."

Munira's eyes welled up with tears again, and Farayeh realized that with these deaths, Inas's sister and he would be perpetually linked by the horror of what they had witnessed in the run-down apartment in Old Amman.

"When did you last speak with your sister?" Farayeh asked.

"Thursday evening," Munira said. "She was going to come to my doctor's appointment with me Monday morning. I wanted her to bring the kids over Friday after my husband went to the mosque, but she said the baby had a fever, and she wasn't feeling well either. She didn't want to get me sick." At this, she rubbed her round belly and let out a sob.

Mansour looked askance at Farayeh. "And the other children? Did she mention if they were also ill?"

"No, just Omar, the baby, but I joked with her that they would all get sick eventually. Children, you know? There's no way to keep them apart."

Farayeh took down Munira's recollection of the phone call; it would help establish the time of death, and he made a note to mention it to the coroner. "Back at the apartment, you mentioned that you thought someone killed them. Talk to us about that."

A wave of anger rushed over Munira's face, draining her of the slight colour she had. "Yes," she said, her voice agitated. "It was her husband – soon to be former husband. I know he had a hand in this!"

"You say former – they are estranged?"

"She had enough of his abuse. Layth was controlling in every way. He even checked my phone messages to her – her own sister! Who does this to a woman? And then she confided in me after the baby was born that he had been hitting her, kicking her. I begged my husband to help her, but he didn't want all of those children moving in with us. And look what happened!" She broke down into sobs again.

"I know this is difficult," Farayeh said. "You are doing very well. Layth is his name?"

"Yes, Layth Mohammed El Ali."

"How long had she been living apart from him?"

"Since August when school started," she said. "Inas wanted the older boys to be distracted by school so they wouldn't be so hurt by the upcoming divorce."

"How did her husband take Inas leaving him? You said he was controlling."

"He was furious. She said he would show up at her apartment at all hours, banging on the door, threatening to take the children from her. She showed me the texts he sent her, too. He told her he was going to kill her, but I never thought he would hurt the children." Munira broke down, and Mansour handed her a box of tissues.

"Do you have his number? Where would he be right now?"

"Probably at work if not at home. He's a manager at Carrefour Madina."

"Think carefully. Is there anyone else who would want to harm your sister and her children?"

"No, no one. If not Layth, it would be his family. He's very manipulative, and they would definitely help him to preserve his honour."

"I see. I'm going to follow up on the phone call to your husband, Munira. Come, *habibti*, we'll walk you up front so you can wait for him and get another cup of tea. If you think of anything else, here is my card." Farayeh slid his card across the table to the distraught woman.

"Please," she said as she hoisted herself out of her chair. "Please, you have to arrest him!"

"Don't worry," Mansour said. "We will find out whoever is responsible and bring him to justice."

Once they had escorted Munira to the front and made sure her husband was contacted, Farayeh and Mansour sent patrol officers to collect the husband from his work or home. They then turned their attention to the Egyptian landlord, who was waiting impatiently in interview room one. He had a small paper cup of coffee in front of him – empty, presumably, as he was in the midst of putting a cigarette butt into the cup.

"*Kaif haluk*," Fayareh said as he slid into a chair across from the Egyptian. "Sorry to keep you waiting."

"I hope this won't take too long," Marwan said. "I knew I shouldn't have rented to that woman with all of her children. A respectable mother wouldn't break up her family."

"A desperate mother would have little choice," Mansour said, the annoyance clear in his tone. The Egyptian shrugged and pulled another cigarette from his pack on the table.

"How long had Ms. Inas and her children been in your building?" Farayeh began.

"Her lease started in the middle of August," Marwan said. "She asked me not to charge her until the Monday, but she had begun moving things in over the weekend, so I told her, no, it wasn't possible to give her a free weekend. I have bills to pay, too, you know? I was worried she wouldn't make the rent payment on time, but she was never late. Now with what happened in that apartment, I doubt I will ever be able to rent it again. Such a waste!"

"I assume you mean the loss of a young mother and four children?" Mansour said.

Farayeh could feel his partner bristling next to him. Farayeh was also disgusted by the landlord's attitude, but he needed any information the man could provide and so kept his composure.

Marwan took a heavy drag from his cigarette and met Mansour's disapproving look with another shrug. "*Inshallah*," he said after a moment.

"Did she have any visitors?"

"No, not really. Only that pushy sister of hers. She kept to herself."

"I understand her estranged husband would occasionally harass her," Farayeh said.

"Yes, but he wasn't what you would consider a visitor. He would come and pound on her door. Such a racket! The rest of my tenants would complain every time he came to her apartment."

"Did she let him in on these occasions?"

"I don't think so. They would argue loudly in the hallway. I had to threaten to call the police on at least four occasions."

"Did you find him threatening?"

"As much as any angry man can be," Marwan said. "He wasn't happy with her, if that's what you mean. He screamed about her breaking up their family, embarrassing him."

"When was the last time you witnessed such an encounter?"

"A little over a week ago. He showed up on a Friday after *maghrib* prayer. I remember this because the *adhan* was sounding in the neighbourhood. I found it rude that they would carry on like this during the evening prayer."

"Could you overhear any of their conversation?"

"What, do you think me an old woman, listening at the doorway? It's not my business. I told them to take their argument inside or I would call the police again."

"And did they?"

"Did they what?"

"Did they go inside?"

"No, no. The husband cursed us both and left. Every time I saw him, he was angry with her."

"Did he have a key to the apartment?"

"No, and I wouldn't have given one to him even if he had asked. I only have two copies. She had one, and I have the master copy. I charge tenants extra for multiple copies, so she never requested more than one."

"And your previous tenant in that apartment returned the keys to you?"

"They always return my keys. I charge fifty JD if they don't, for my time and effort and the cost."

Mansour looked at Farayeh, suppressing a smirk. It was clear to both detectives that this landlord was both a penny pincher and a scoundrel – as indeed many landlords were in Old Amman.

"What about a handyman? Did she let someone like that in who may have gained access to her apartment?"

"What handyman?" the Egyptian puffed up. "When something breaks, I am the handyman."

"Is there any other way to gain access to the apartment other than the front door?"

"Maybe if you are a spider and can crawl up the building and into a window."

"Is there anything else you can think of – no matter how insignificant it might seem – that we should know?" Farayeh asked.

"No, nothing. Am I free to go?"

"Yes," the detective said. "Please write down your number here. We may need to access the apartment again, so please leave it locked and untouched until I call you to release it."

"*Sah, sah*," Marwan said. He grunted as he stood up and slid his cigarettes into his pocket. "You know where to find me, *ya basha*."

With that, the detectives led him out of the interview room and watched him head back out into the cold and rain.

It was right after the *zuhr* prayer when Layth El Ali was escorted into the Criminal Investigation Unit offices. His eyes were wild, his hair raised upward from his scalp, as if he had been pulling it on his ride to the station.

"No tears," Mansour whispered to Farayeh as they watched him enter investigation room number one.

"He may be in shock," Farayeh murmured. "Let's see what he has to say."

When the detectives walked into the interview room, Layth's expression changed very little. A tall, lanky man, he was wearing tight grey slacks with a white shirt. He had loosened the red tie around his neck, so that the overall impression he made was one of dishevelment.

"I'm Detective Farayeh. Can we get you anything?" Farayeh asked. "You must be cold without a coat."

"I didn't think to bring one," Layth responded quietly. He looked at the detective, but Farayeh felt as if the man were looking through him, not at him.

"Brother, let me first say on behalf of Detective Mansor and myself that we are very sorry for your loss. I take it the officers informed you of the tragedy that has unfolded with your family. *Hasabi Allah*."

"Surely this is a mistake," Layth said. "Please, they cannot all be gone!"

The detectives gauged his reaction intently. "I wish it were not so, brother," Mansour said. "We need to talk to you about what happened. When was the last time you saw your estranged wife and children."

Layth looked at Mansour sullenly. "I don't like this word estranged. We were trying to work out our differences."

"That's not what I asked you," Mansour said sternly. "When did you see them last?"

"I'm not sure," Layth said. "I tried to go visit the kids at least once a week, but Inas was so stubborn!"

"Witnesses said you were at her place last Friday evening and that you were arguing."

"That could be," the man admitted. "I've been so busy with work and trying to manage a household on my own that I cannot recall the exact day."

Farayeh looked askance at his partner. "You expect us to believe that you cannot remember the day you last saw your children?"

Mouth agog, Layth stared at him briefly before answering. "I would have to look at my work schedule. I cover for a lot of people."

"How would you describe your relationship with Inas?" Farayeh asked.

"Strained, I guess you could say? She was always worried about money and the children. We had very little time alone together."

"Have you ever gotten violent with her?" Mansour asked pointedly.

Layth looked uncomfortable with the question and hesitated in answering. "If I did, it was only because she was out of line and yelling. Sometimes a man has to remind his wife who is in charge."

"It seems to me you provoked her by going to her apartment and arguing in public with her," Mansour said. "There are plenty of witnesses that told us you went over to her place on multiple occasions and caused a scene. I understand the police were even called out."

"Yes, but I didn't hit her then. That Egyptian who owns the building wouldn't even let me get a word in before calling the police. And I wasn't that loud – you are speaking louder to me now that I was with my wife."

"Is it possible you got frustrated with your wife for not letting you see the children last Friday, and you went too far?" Farayeh asked. He leaned in closer to the suspect.

"Ridiculous," Layth said. "You think I would kill my own children? You are a very poor detective."

Mansour reached across the table and slapped the man quickly, leaving a red welt on his face. Shocked by the detective's aggression, Layth tipped his chair back against the wall. His expression was a mixture of anger and fear.

"*Sharmoot*," Mansour said, his voice heated. "Here your wife and children are murdered, and you have no emotions, nothing but contempt for the men trying to find justice for them. I'm going to ask you again: what did you do at their apartment last Friday evening?"

"I already told you. I wanted to see the children, but Inas wouldn't let me."

"What time were you there?"

"I don't remember – ask your witnesses."

Mansour looked tempted to slap him again, but Farayeh held him back. "We have," Farayeh said. "We understand you were there at 10 in the evening–a little late to visit young children."

"The witnesses said you also smelled strongly of alcohol," Mansour said disapprovingly.

"I do not usually drink," Layth insisted. "But since my wife left with the children, the house was too quiet and sad. I would drink to put myself to sleep."

"Were you in the habit of drinking before your wife took the kids and left you?"

"No – not very often."

"How often?"

"I don't know. Maybe once or twice a month when work was very difficult."

"There is a lot you don't seem to know, brother," Mansour said. "Perhaps you should not drink if it affects your memory."

"I must tell you," Farayeh interjected. "I find it strange you are not weeping or angry for your wife and children. My wife just recently gave birth to our son, and I could not imagine behaving as you are."

"You can judge me when your whole family is wiped out at once."

"We can judge you without experiencing the same tragedy," Mansour said. "And my partner makes a very good observation. We haven't seen you shed.

one tear for your wife or children, and you just received the news. What kind of man are you that you can be so cold?"

"I don't know what you want from me," Layth said. "If I wept and screamed and tore off my shirt, you would accuse me of being dramatic. I don't know why I cannot cry right now. I still don't believe this is real. It just can't be."

"It is, and you know it is," Farayeh said. "We wouldn't bring you in on some cruel joke. No detective would waste his time like this."

"And you are wasting *our* time," Mansour said. "The only person with any reason to harm Inas and her children is you. You have hurt her before and threatened her openly. We have plenty of witnesses to attest to your behaviour."

"I don't know what to tell you," Layth said quietly. "I really don't."

"It's not difficult," Farayeh said. "Tell us the truth."

At that, Layth put his head down on the table and refused to look up at the detectives.

"We're going to step out for a moment," Farayeh said, motioning to Mansour. "I will bring you a coffee. You should pray almighty Allah helps you to do the right thing."

Once they left the room, Mansour rubbed his palm across his face in frustration. "I know he did it."

"Well, he is certainly the only suspect we have at the moment. What are your thoughts? Should we keep at him today?"

Mansour looked at his watch. "I think we let him sit in a cell and stare at a blank wall overnight. We have 48 hours, and he may be a suicide risk. He doesn't seem either remorseful or even completely aware of what he's done."

"Good thinking," Farayeh said. "After the nightmare we've seen today, I want to go home and see my wife and son and tell them I love them."

When Farayeh returned to the offices the following morning, the red message light on his phone was blinking. He hit play to hear the serious voice of the coroner, Dr. Kahled Haddad, entreating him to come to the Al Basheer hospital morgue as soon as he could.

Farayeh called his partner on his cell phone to find out how close he was to arriving. "Five minutes," Mansour said. "I'm about to pull onto Al-Hareth. You want me to drive?"

"Sure," Farayeh said. "I'll head downstairs now."

Mansour was true to his word and pulled up in front of the office in six minutes. The rain was still coming down from the storm front that hit Amman the day before, so Farayeh jumped into the car as quickly as he could.

The men greeted each other but sat through much of the ride in silence, Fayareh looking over his notes on the case, Mansour angrily struggling against the impatient city drivers made even more impatient by the rain and cold. "What are all these idiots doing out in this weather?" the detective mused. Farayeh was smart enough to realize the question was rhetorical and also smart enough not to answer and further annoy his partner.

What was usually a fifteen-minute drive took a little over a half hour in the weather and morning traffic, so that the pair pulled up to the coroner's office a little after 9 a.m. After checking in, they headed to Dr. Haddad's office only to find he was in his usual spot: the morgue. They doubled back and took the stairwell down to find the doctor at work, cracking open the rib cage of a middle-aged man.

"*Marhaba*," he said as he saw the detectives swing through the doors. He set down the rib shears beside the deceased man's greyish arm. "Let me show you what I've found."

Farayeh didn't know Haddad to be a sentimental man, but the coroner had grouped the five bodies of the Old Amman murders together on their gurneys. He delicately pulled back the sheet covering Inas. Farayeh was relieved he hadn't revealed the bodies of the children. The sight of their small frames covered by sheets was troubling enough.

"Come," the coroner said. "Let's take a look."

The two men approached reverently; where the doctor approached his work scientifically, the detectives were somehow further removed from death's face and thus more hesitant. Inas's body was cut down the centre.

"I worked on the children yesterday but wanted to share my findings on her with you this morning," Haddad said. "So, I have just opened her up."

The trio peered into her chest and abdomen, and Haddad used a gloved hand to lift one of Inas's lungs. "See?"

Although Farayeh and Mansour had a combined fifteen years of experience between them, they could not tell what the coroner was pointing out and looked at him quizzically. Haddad frowned at them as if they were schoolboys confused by simple arithmetic. "*Ya-zelmeh*," he said. "Come, gentlemen. You have been in my workroom before and seen many bodies. What is different here?"

Farayeh stared at the lungs and heart, the liver and realized what Haddad was pointing out. "Bright red!" he said brightly. "What caused this, Doctor?"

"The results of the lab work will take another two weeks," the coroner said. "But this colouring of the organs is a telltale sign of carbon monoxide poisoning. All of the bodies have the same discoloration of the organs."

Farayeh gave Mansour a sideways look. "Intentional poisoning?" Mansour asked.

"That I cannot say as I was not at the crime scene."

"I think we better go back and look for the source," Farayeh said. "*Shukran jazeera*, brother."

"Look for any pipes connected to gas systems," the coroner advised. "And please, leave me a message if you find anything unusual. I would like to know if my hunch is right."

While the weather wasn't any better on the return from their meeting with Haddad, the traffic had eased, so the drive back was less congested. Mansour was still not in a talkative mood, his mind likely preoccupied with what the detectives would uncover back at the Old Amman apartment. Farayeh was similarly consumed by his own thoughts and occasionally scribbled in his notebook. The only sounds during the drive were the patter of rainfall on the windowpanes and roof of the car, and Farayeh's brief phone call instructing the landlord to meet them at Inas's apartment.

"*Marhaba*," Marwan said when he saw them climbing the stairs. "I've already unlocked it for you." Although it was almost eleven, the landlord smelled strongly of cigarettes. Farayeh found himself wondering how many the man had already smoked so early into the day.

The Egyptian opened the door and escorted the pair into the apartment, which still had the faint, sickly sweet scent of death in it coupled with the strong, clinical scent of pine someone had used to try to eliminate the smell. "I will leave you to it," he said, but Farayeh stopped him.

"We may need you," the detective said. "I notice it's cold in here. Where is the heater?"

The landlord led the pair to a small door in the hallway and slid open a bolt. "She was complaining about the heater not working, so I fixed it myself and added the lock. I didn't trust that her younger kids would leave it alone."

Farayeh squatted down and pulled his Maglite from his belt while Mansour leaned in to watch. In the small cubby was a canister attached to a heating unit that looked like it had been refurbished many times over the years. Fayareh reached for the canister and slid it toward him, surprised by how light it was. "I think it's empty," he said.

"Not possible," Marwan snipped. "I just replaced it recently for her when I fixed the heater. She insisted it was my responsibility as she hadn't used it before her lease started. We argued back and forth on this –"

As the detective slid the canister out of the cupboard, the hose connecting it to the heater popped off immediately with no tension. Farayeh looked up over his shoulder at his partner, the two sharing a knowing look. "I'll call forensics to come back," Mansour said, pulling his cell phone from his pocket.

"What? What is it?" the landlord asked, his voice elevated.

Farayeh stood up and looked down at him. "I'm afraid we've likely found our killer, Mr. El Shebini," he said sadly. "Come, let's step outside to wait for the forensics team, and I'll explain."

AUTHOR BIOGRAPHY

Southern by the grace of grits, Moxie is an avid horror and crime fan and writer who lives with a very patient rescue mutt, a very assertive (former) street cat who beats up the very patient mutt, and one very patient partner who encourages her in all her goals. She has lived in Texas, Louisiana, and Tennessee and loves the South, despite its flaws. Moxie is the recipient of the 2021 Al Sadeqqi Writing Fellowship and was fortunate to complete *The Seven* under the mentorship of brilliant UK crime writer Mark Billingham. She is represented by Luigi Bonomi of LBA.

The Gardener

by Michael Lynes

••••

As I turn on the coffee machine a low muttering filters through the closed blinds from the garden. I hear Tariq talking on his mobile every morning at 6.00am. He lets himself into the garden through the door that opens out onto the road. He reaches over the top of the door to take the key we leave hanging on the inside. It's 7.00am where his family are. He's talking to his children before they go to school, which starts at 7.30am in Pakistan. I know because I Googled it.

The coffee machine gurgles and hisses as it prepares my customary creamy double espresso. I twist open the blinds. Tariq is squatting, cradling the phone to his ear with one hand, whilst spraying my lawn with a hose in the other. For most of the year it's so hot he waters it twice a day. I'm not normally back from work when he comes in the evening. Sarah usually was though – when she was here. If he misses more than three days, the grass begins to shrivel and die.

Tariq's thick brown hair is always immaculately combed and oiled. The neatly trimmed moustache gives him a military bearing. Perhaps he was in the army. His skin has turned mahogany brown from spending so much time in the sun. He's developed a paunch lately – probably too much bread and rice. I close the blind before he notices me. I sip my coffee standing with my back to the window.

I'm worried about the brown patch beneath the hedge in the far lefthand corner of the lawn. I've pointed it out to Tariq and told him to give it extra water. If his English was better, we could discuss other remedies – compost, fertilizer or something. He just looks at me and says, "Inshallah." It's not God who needs to be willing, it's him. Sarah always got on with him better than I did. Perhaps I should just put one of those ridiculous garden statues on top of the patch to hide it. He always listens to me attentively as his dark brown eyes scan my face searching for clues to mitigate his poor understanding. I speak in a sort of pidgin English, which seems to help. He calls me, "Sir." I tried to teach him my name once, but he couldn't get his tongue around, "James." It came out as, "Jams." On the one occasion I engaged him in a personal conversation I think he said that he'd been in Dubai for more than ten years. Almost the same amount of time as Sarah and me. He's here like thousands of others: to earn a better life for his family.

I finish my coffee, rinse the cup, and put it in the dishwasher. I part the blinds and peer out. Tariq is smiling. His son or his daughter must be telling him something that delights him. In the cooler months, when I can leave the kitchen window ajar, I hear fragments of his conversation. I don't understand it as I don't know any Urdu. But I catch the tone and glimpse his downcast expression. Sometimes I hear a young child talking loudly and occasionally crying. I can't believe that Tariq enjoys being here. He wants to be with his son, his daughter, his wife in Lahore, Karachi or Faisalabad, wherever they live. But every morning, promptly at 6am, he carries out this nurturing ritual to provide sustenance for my lawn and his family. To prevent both from withering.

Sarah and I relocated from Manchester a decade ago. My job selling insurance was going nowhere. An old school friend offered me a job managing an insurance broker's office in downtown Dubai. It was a prestigious firm owned by some eminent citizens, so I was happy to take the plunge. Sarah wasn't sure about giving up her teaching assistant job at our local primary. She loved the kids and the school. But I kept on at her about the benefits to my career and the big salary. Eventually she gave in. My friend assured her she would easily get another position in Dubai. She looked for a job and was offered one, but I dissuaded her from accepting it. We didn't need the money; I was earning enough. I convinced her that she'd be better off relaxing, making friends and taking care of the villa and the garden. She had no family – she was an only child and her parents died in a car crash when she was twelve. There were some aunts and uncles in Scotland and Australia, but she stopped contacting them after we married. I told her there wasn't much point, we were never going to see them.

At first, I loved Dubai. If you're in your thirties, why wouldn't you? It's a safe but exciting city that seems to be at the centre of the world. You can enjoy a luxurious lifestyle and afford to travel. But as I entered my forties things changed. Dubai is a city for the young, not washed-up expats like us. "Give it one more year," was the refrain around the golf club bar. Some of them had managed to cling on by their fingernails to the same job for thirty years. Were they too scared to go home? Institutionalised? Perhaps they really were happy, and the problem was me.

Sarah seemed happy. She didn't have many friends, but she kept fit, learnt how to cook, and even started writing. I asked to see her stories, but she said she was embarrassed because they were rubbish. I tried opening the files on her laptop but couldn't work out the password. Then she said she wanted children. I wasn't enthusiastic but was willing to go through the motions. We tried for a few years, but we failed. When I say we, it was me. Low sperm motility apparently. Bit of a blow to my ego, but part of me was relieved. I didn't want the responsibility. But Sarah was devastated when I told her. At first there was confusion on her face, then her eyes tightened, and she pinched her lips. For a moment I thought I saw pure malice. Then she brightened, clasped my hand, and muttered something about IVF or adoption. I wasn't convinced and neither of us ever said or did anything about it. That's when I first noticed the vacancy behind Sarah's eyes.

She'd been much better at dealing with Tariq than me. I used to peer at them through the slats of the blinds as they chatted in the garden. His face always lit up when she went out to give him a cup of tea. Not many blonde women in Pakistan I suppose. He didn't seem to have a problem understanding her. Tariq took better care of the garden when Sarah had been around. Did she communicate more effectively, or did he just do the job he was supposed to because she smiled and gave him tea and cake?

One day I'd come home a little earlier than usual. I turned the key in the front door and entered quietly. I wanted to surprise Sarah. I heard the toilet flush from the downstairs bathroom and waited for her to come out. But Tariq opened the door. I stared at him. This had never happened before. He'd never entered the house, let alone the bathroom. There was no reason for him to do so.

'Madam,' Tariq said pointing behind me.

Sarah came down the stairs. She must have seen the surprise in my face as she said, "Oh, for goodness' sake," and muttered something in Urdu to Tariq. He bowed his head at me and went back out to the garden. She told me he'd needed to use the toilet as he had a stomach-ache.

I said, 'Urdu?' and went upstairs to change.

Yesterday afternoon I'd just fixed my second gin and tonic and was about to turn on the Manchester City match – it was a lunchtime kick-off in the UK so 4:30 in Dubai – when the doorbell rang. It was around two weeks after Sarah had disappeared. I flung open the door expecting to see yet another delivery guy trying to drop something at the wrong villa. It was two policemen. Finally.

The taller one said, 'Mr James Carmichael?'

I nodded.

'Good evening, sir. Sergeant Khaled.' He held out his identity card.

As I took it, he arched an eyebrow. He obviously wasn't used to people studying it. But you can never be too careful. Satisfied, I returned it, and asked how I could help.

'It's about the report you made, sir. Last week. At the Smart Police Station?'

These small buildings had sprung up all over Dubai recently. They were very convenient, there was one just around the corner from my villa. They were unmanned and after popping your national identity card into a machine you could do all sorts of things: pay traffic fines, file a criminal complaint, get a corpse entry permit, and report a missing wife.

I invited them in. They took off their peaked caps and I gestured towards the dining table in front of the door that led to the garden. The sergeant positioned himself at one end of the table and took out an electronic tablet and a stylus. His colleague sat to his left and crossed his legs. He had not introduced himself or offered his identity card. The epaulettes on his shoulders were different to Khaled's. He must be of a higher rank. I placed a glass of water in front of each of them. Khaled nodded and said, "Shukran." I sat at the opposite end of the table. The other policeman stared steadily out into the garden and evaded my attempts to make eye contact.

Khaled took a sip of water and began. 'Last week you reported your wife was missing. Is that correct?'

'Yes. To be honest, I'd expected you to respond more quickly.'

I saw Khaled glance at his colleague – no, clearly his superior – who was tapping a forefinger on his bottom lip. Still staring out into the garden. He jutted his chin at the sergeant, who continued. 'We're surprised you made an electronic report and made no attempt to follow up.'

I was silent for a long moment.

The two men waited me out. Khaled pecked at the tablet with the stylus. 'Sarah and I – you must be married men yourselves. I'm sure you

understand.' My smile was not returned by either of them. 'We'd been having

some difficulties. She'd discovered she couldn't have children. You know how women get about that.' Still no reaction. 'I thought she'd taken herself off for a few days.'

'Yet you reported her missing?' Khaled said with a smile.

'As a precaution.'

'Precaution? An odd word.' Khaled said.

His superior took a sip of water.

'I thought I was following the law. She might have absconded. She's here under my sponsorship.'

'Did you contact her employer?'

'She doesn't work.'

'What about her relatives back home in the UK?'

'There's nobody. She's an only child and an orphan.'

'We spoke to your neighbours,' Khaled said. He held my gaze for a long moment. 'What do you think they told us?'

Shit. I glanced at Khaled's superior. He got up and stood in front of the door to the garden. I shook my head and shrugged.

Khaled glanced down at the tablet and read, 'We heard loud fights and slamming doors.' He paused. 'It has gotten worse in the past few weeks.'

It had since the incident with Tariq. I said nothing.

Khaled said, 'Out of respect to your employers we've conducted this ... discussion ... in your home. But perhaps we should continue this at the police station.'

I heard the back door to the garden slam. Tariq had arrived.

'I want a lawyer. Perhaps you should speak to the gardener.'

Khaled's superior turned to me and said, 'We already have.'

My lawyer is a well-spoken and very expensive guy from India. He says that if we can convince the judge that it was a crime of passion,

I might escape the death penalty. We need to play up the affair with the gardener. I'd thought that in the absence of a body the police wouldn't be able to mount a case. I'd told them the truth. When Sarah disappeared, I thought she was annoyed with me and needed some time alone. If I'm honest I'd enjoyed being by myself. I could watch the football in peace. But after a week when she didn't respond to my calls or texts, I thought I'd better report her missing. She's my legal responsibility in this country.

They dug up the garden looking for her and ruined Tariq's lawn. They were very interested in the brown patch beneath the hedge in the far lefthand corner of the lawn. I did tell them they wouldn't find anything. But there's so much circumstantial evidence. The neighbours' testimony for one. They'd been through her laptop and read her short stories which were all about abused women and so called, "coercive control." What's fiction got to do with real life, for God's sake? Tariq told them he'd witnessed me shouting at her. And he'd seen some marks on her face. I never touched her. Why would they listen to a gardener? I told the police it was him.

That's when they produced the letter he'd given them. From Sarah to, "Whom it may concern, in the event of my disappearance." I'd had to admit it did look like her handwriting. My lawyer says the expert analysis is very convincing. She wrote that she'd given it to Tariq because she trusted him. She predicted that I would try to blame him and didn't want him to be under any suspicion. But the lies! I never hit her. All that shit about me controlling her. *She* wanted to leave Manchester; I didn't force her. I didn't stop her from seeing her relatives. I can't help it if she's not very good at making friends.

If I'm lucky they'll transfer me out of Dubai after a few years and

Arabian Noir

I'll spend the rest of my life in a British jail. But I didn't do it. It *was* bloody Tariq. He must have tried it on with Sarah, she refused, and it got out of hand. I warned her about getting too friendly with the likes of him. He probably wrapped the garden hose around her neck and strangled her. Then got some of his mates to help him dispose of her. They could have hidden a body in a truck amidst all the garden detritus and disposed of it at the dump.

Nobody else believes me but you do. Don't you?

Aisha squealed so loudly when I gave her the good news that I had to hold the phone away from my ear. I didn't tell her the truth about where the money came from. I told her I'd been tending the garden of a Russian billionaire's villa on the weekend, and he'd given me a huge tip. She was so relieved that we didn't have to worry about Danyal and Ameerah's school fees anymore.

But it was Miss Sarah who gave me the money. She was always kind to me. Bringing me tea and cake and asking after my family. She even learnt enough Urdu to speak to them once or twice. Miss Sarah didn't deserve to be treated that way by her husband. I heard him shouting at her and she confided in me that he did it all the time. She said he was always trying to control her and stop her from seeing her friends. He was sneaky as well. I didn't like the way he spied on me from the kitchen. Standing there drinking his coffee, looking down on me. He thought I didn't notice. And he even spoke to me in broken English. Just because I don't speak it that well doesn't mean I don't understand it. I'm not stupid.

When she told me she wanted to leave him I said why not get a divorce. Miss Sarah said he would make things difficult by employing expensive lawyers who would drag it out for years. She planned to escape and asked me to help. I knew people from my army days who knew people who could make a fake passport good enough to get her out of Dubai. He wouldn't know where she'd gone. I was happy to help but told her it would be expensive. She paid me and added twenty per cent on top for me to keep. I tried to refuse but she said her parents had left her money. She'd hidden it from her husband as he would have wasted it. They came to Dubai in the first place because of the debts he had in the UK. Miss Sarah looked so sad when she realised she had never trusted him.

She wouldn't tell me exactly where she was going. She did say it was an island where she would swim every day and teach English to small children. The same age as Danyal and Ameerah. Miss Sarah gave me a letter. She made me promise that I would only give it to the police if her husband made any trouble. She told me I was a good man and hugged me. Aisha would not approve so I didn't tell her that part of the story.

About a week after Miss Sarah left, the police came to her villa and arrested me. They were a little rough with me at first. But I trusted Miss Sarah and I gave them the letter. They tested it and then accepted I didn't have anything to do with her disappearance and let me go.

I think of Miss Sarah often. I imagine the smiling faces of her students. And I give thanks to Allah for what she has done for my children. I hope she has found peace. And I know she will keep her promise to visit me and my family in Faisalabad. One day soon. Inshallah.

AUTHOR BIOGRAPHY

Michael writes the historical thriller series, *The Isaac Alvarez Mysteries*. The third book in the series, *The Red Citadel*, was published in 2023; the first, *Blood Libel*, won a prize at the 2020 Emirates Literature Festival. Michael is chair of the Gulf Chapter of the Crime Writers' Association. He's a member of the Historical Novel Society, for which he regularly reviews. He's originally from London, but currently lives in Dubai with his family. You can find out more at www.michaellynes.com and follow him on Twitter: @MLynesauthor

Dubai Heat

A Director Dudka story by Alex Shaw

◆◆◆◆

Security Service of Ukraine (SBU) Headquarters, Volodymyrska Street, Kyiv

Gennady Dudka fanned the contents of the envelope out across his scarred, leather-topped desk. Postmarked Dubai, the letter had arrived that morning. It had a ragged edge, seemingly torn from a reporter's pad, the Russian text read *'Dear Genna, You must act on this! – O.K.'*

Dudka wrinkled his brow and again studied the documents. They were damning, but were they real? As the director of the SBU's Anti-Corruption & Organised Crime Directorate it was essential he found out.

A knock and then the oversized wooden door creaked as it opened to reveal Vitaly Blazhevich. "You wanted to see me?"

"You need to postpone your holiday." Dudka tapped his desk with an index finger. "Look at this."

Blazhevich took a chair and pulled the assorted papers and photographs towards him. Bewilderment and then shock registered on the young agent's face. "This is unbelievable, yet..."

"What?"

"Yet I believe Poltavets is capable of this." Blazhevich picked up a photograph and blew out his cheeks. "If this is real, we have an SBU agent planting something on the underside of a vehicle, which later exploded killing a journalist."

"Yes." The murder of Anton Haymenko had happened six months before. Dudka's ongoing investigation had failed to turn up any actionable leads on what was the most high-profile assassination of a reporter in more than a decade. The SBU as a whole and Dudka, in particular, were under immense pressure.

Blazhevich said, "Poltavets was promoted and transferred here by Director Zlotnik."

"And reports directly to him," Dudka added.

"This implicates Zlotnik."

"It does." Dudka allowed a smile to wander across his face. He disliked the Head of the SBU - Director Yuri Zlotnik. The enmity was reciprocated. Zlotnik was two decades his junior, ambitious, patronising and had close ties with previous Russian facing presidential administrations.

"Do you know who sent this?" Blazevich asked.

"I have no idea."

Blazhevich reread the note. "Are the sender's initials O.K. or are they asking you if you are, O.K.?"

Dudka shrugged. "Why write in Russian then use an English phrase? Find out if these photographs have been tampered with in any way."

"I will, but I can't be 100% sure without the original files. The metadata would help."

"I see," Dudka didn't. He wasn't sure what exactly metadata was. "And check the bank account given here. Is it real, who opened it, who made these deposits, and who can access it." Dudka gazed across the desk at his protégé, "My daughter and granddaughter live in Dubai."

Blazhevich's eyes darted to the envelope, he understood the implication. "Is it a message?"

"Is it a threat," Dudka leant back in his chair, it creaked, "that the sender knows where my family live?"

"You should phone your daughter."

Dudka agreed. "This stays between you and me, a closed investigation."

"I understand."

Blazhevich collected the documents and exited. Dudka retrieved his iPhone, pressed his daughter's contact details and held the device to his ear. He moved to the window. Three floors below a grubby yellow trolleybus glided uphill, moving faster than the traffic along the cobbled street. It was the Friday morning before the 'Kyiv Day' holiday weekend and by mid-afternoon, the nearby streets would be busy with locals and tourists. Dudka looked forward to the grand firework display on Independence Square, his daughter especially had always loved that.

"Gennady Stepanovich." Dudka's boss addressed him using his patronym.

Dudka ended his call before it connected and replied in the same manner. "I didn't hear you knock, Yuri Ruslanovich."

Zlotnik hadn't, as was his custom. He sat without being invited to do so. "There is a meeting of the National Security and Defence Council today. As you are well aware, the President is expecting an update on the Haymenko case."

"Is he?"

"Yes. He is." Zlotnik became annoyed, the nostrils in his angular nose flared. "Please tell me you have something new I can tell him?"

Time and experience had taught Dudka caution. "I am working on a potential new lead."

"Meaning? An imminent arrest? Is that what you are saying?"

"I'd can't elaborate, yet."

Zlotnik paused a beat before he spoke. "More so now than ever before the world is watching us. Unless we show the President real progress, I am afraid there will be consequences."

"I see."

"Do you? You are the longest-serving Director in the history of the SBU and whilst your achievements are many, you have done little to solve this case. Questions are being asked, and I can only defend your position for so long. Do I make myself clear?"

"Exceptionally so."

"Results are all I ask for." Zlotnik stalked out of the office.

Dudka watched him go, hoping he'd trip on the threadbare rug. Why the sudden interest in the Haymenko case? Dudka sighed, then called his daughter using WhatsApp. There was a pause before it connected, she had told him this was something to do with a VPN, but he didn't quite understand what that was.

"Allo! Papa!" His daughter's voice was as clear in his ear as though she was standing in the next room and not the next continent.

"How are you, my sonichka?" Dudka always called her his little 'sun'. It was something his wife has started, and he had continued.

"Press the video button so I can show you where we are."

"You're not at home?"

"No."

Dudka frowned, removed the phone from his ear and fiddled with it. Eventually he managed to get a video image. What he saw was his daughter and granddaughter waving at him from what looked like a high balcony. "Zaichik!", Little Rabbit – he called his granddaughter, "Where are you and mummy?"

"On holiday, Didys."

"But you live on holiday!"

"It's called a staycation, Didys."

"Ah, I see."

His granddaughter took the phone from her mother, "We're in Atlantis."

"Ah, the mystical lost city."

"No, the hotel." She moved the camera to show the panorama below them. "Look, there's the beach, and the palm and the monorail."

"Ah," Dudka said, "that makes more sense."

Zankovetskaya Street, Kyiv

Dudka's radio, like him, was old and refused to retire. He ate lunch as an orchestra played a tune he half recognised. Dudka wasn't an aficionado, but his wife had been. He still missed Irina, especially so at weekends. They'd met on a Sunday at an open-air recital in Mariinski Park when he was a young, idealistic KGB officer; they married a month later and honeymooned in Yalta.

Dudka, Irina and their daughter Katya had been happy in the large flat on Zankovetskaya Street, the home he now shared with only his memories. His daughter having moved to Dubai with her daughter, had urged him to retire and join them, but Dudka stayed put. Katya had a villa in a development grandly named 'Victory Heights'. It had a large, tear drop shaped swimming pool and the back garden overlooked a golf course. He'd visited a couple of times and although he understood why others loved the place, he found Dubai too hot, too modern, and too busy. He preferred the Kyiv heat.

The orchestra continued. He often listened to music whilst he ate, a doctor recommended he do so to aid his digestion. An electronic ringing interrupted the orchestra, his iPhone. He ignored it and continued to slurp his borsch. Dudka made the beetroot soup every Saturday, it was one of the few things he knew how to cook. The ringing stopped but now his landline trilled. Dudka never ignored his house phone, so few knew the number. He turned the volume down on the radio and shuffled across the kitchen. "Yes?"

"Genna is that you?"

"Who is this?" Dudka didn't recognise the voice.

"It's Oleg. Oleg Philipovich."

Dudka frowned. "Oleg Philipovich?"

"Oleg Philipovich Komarov."

Dudka was surprised. "It's been a long time."

"Your secretary gave me this number."

"Oh, did she?"

"I rang last night but you weren't in."

"That's because I was out."

"Did you get my envelope? I did sign it."

"You did?" Dudka sat; his soup was rapidly cooling.

"What do you think?"

Arabian Noir

What did he think? Dudka was silent, the line hummed, was this the mystery envelope? "Where did you post it from?"

"Dubai."

"You were on holiday?"

"I've retired there."

"Very nice."

"Genna, I'm in Kyiv now, we need to meet."

"Oh?"

"There are things I can't tell you over the phone. Can we meet tomorrow?"

"When and where?"

"Midday at the River Port."

"O.K." Replied Dudka. "Agreed, see you then."

"Agreed." Komarov signed off.

Dudka stirred his tepid borsch as he tried to understand what was happening. He and Oleg Komarov had been in the same KGB Border Guards unit until it merged with other divisions. Both men were then transferred, Dudka to Kyiv and Komarov to his native Moscow. After the Soviet Union vanished the two colleagues found themselves employed by the security services of different countries: Dudka the Ukrainian SBU and Komarov the Russian KGB. Same people, new hats. Dudka slurped his soup. To his recollection, he and Komarov had never been close, but time, age and distance habitually turned acquaintances into friends; now that they were both in their seventies, he imagined that made them 'old friends'. Indeed, their last meeting, a reunion of sorts over a decade before, had been cordial. But how had Komarov come into possession of evidence regarding his investigation? And how had he obtained his home telephone number, his secretary certainly didn't have it? It made no sense at all. Dudka finished his borsch but as he wiped the bowl clean with a thick chunk of Ukrainski bread, his doorbell rang.

Blazhevich looked tired. Dudka ushered him into the high-ceilinged flat. In the kitchen, he pointed to a chair at the large, oblong table. "What is so important that you've interrupted your Kyiv Day Saturday to see me?"

Blazhevich sat. "I think the documents are real."

Dudka remained standing. He crossed his arms. "Think? We need to know."

"I worked on them most of last night. I'm as sure as I can be, without the original digital files, that the photographs are real."

"The metadata?" Dudka had looked it up.

"Yes. I scanned them, enlarged the edges of the figure we believe is Poltavets and checked for any pixel irregularities, any digital interference."

"You mean joins?"

"Yes. I couldn't see any. And the bank account is real. It belongs to Poltavets. But that's not all. I looked further back for anything else that might be incriminating. Do you remember, he took a holiday last year to Dubai? He stayed at a hotel on the Palm."

"Where the dates come from?"

"I don't know, but he went to Atlantis, a luxury resort and stayed in one of their most exclusive suites. They are reserved for the richest of the rich. The strange part is that there are no records anywhere of him having paid for it."

"Who did?"

"I don't know, but that resort is extremely popular with a certain set of Russians."

"I see." And this time Dudka did. "I need a list of guests who were there at the same time as Poltavets."

"I'm working on that."

Dudka opened the fridge, retrieved a frosted bottle from the freezer compartment and placed it on the table before collecting a pair of shot glasses from the draining board. Without giving Blazhevich a choice, he filled both with vodka. "To success in our investigation. Dudka emptied his glass, Blazhevich did likewise and shuddered. His boss smiled. "How's your wife?"

"Angry with you for postponing her holiday."

"You can have an extra three days added on the end. Now listen, I know who sent me the envelope."

"Who?" Blazhevich asked.

Dudka explained his phone call with Komarov.

"Why choose the river port?"

"Perhaps he wants to take a cruise?" Dudka picked up the bottle and refilled the glasses. "All I know is that Oleg Komarov had our evidence."

Postova Ploshadh Metro Station, Kyiv

Dudka took the short set of stairs up and out of Postova Ploshadh Metro Station. Postova Square was hemmed in on three sides by a busy road that paralleled the Dnipro River and ran through the main street of Kyiv's Podil region. He passed the large McDonald's restaurant which afflicted the square, in his opinion, like a stubborn boil and headed for the river. A pleasant breeze carried from the Dnipro, as he took the walkway up and over the road to join the boardwalk. It was warm. May was the start of the tourist season and he believed, the best time to be in Kyiv, among the myriad of flowering chestnut trees. Dudka navigated his way through the crowds of Kyivites enjoying their Kyiv Day Sunday stroll and strode towards the River Port building. He was ten minutes early but outside Komarov was waiting, eating an ice cream. Unlike Dudka, he'd put on weight since their last meeting but like Dudka he'd retained a full head of white hair.

"Genna!" Komarov seemed jovial. He transferred the cone to his left hand, wiped his right on his trouser leg then offered it to Dudka. "Happy Kyiv Day."

"The same to you, Oleg." Dudka shook the proffered hand, it was sticky. "Are we taking a boat trip?"

"We have tickets for a sailing at 12:10."

Dudka trailed Komarov past the port building to the jetty. Three large, boxy, river boats awaited their passengers. The nearest, which was painted yellow and sky blue to match the Ukrainian national flag, was boarding. Komarov handed a crew member their tickets and was waved towards the gangplank. "We'll sit on the upper deck."

Dudka grunted his consent and after buying beer from the on-board bar, they were seated amidships. Komarov faced the stern and Dudka the bow. A metal table separated the pair.

"It's good to see you, Genna." Komarov raised his beer, his hand exhibiting a slight tremor.

"Likewise, Oleg." They clinked bottles. "You look well."

"Too well," Komarov rubbed his stomach, "retirement makes a man lazy. And it's far too easy to overeat in Dubai. Too many brunches."

The pair of veteran intelligence officers fell silent as a group of twentysomethings passed. They took possession of a table three rows back. The boat's engines fired up as did the entertainment system, further lessening any chance of being overheard. With a backing track of rumbling diesel and mumbling pop music, the ninety-minute cruise started. They pulled away from the jetty and headed south towards the gold-domed Kyiv-Pechersk Lavra monastery.

Dudka wasted no further time with pleasantries. "Why are you here Oleg, and how did you get those documents?"

"Genna you are the only person I trust." Komarov took a mouthful of beer and then started to explain. "My government is trying to destroy yours."

"That's hardly a secret" Dudka replied with scorn.

"But what is a secret is how they are seeking to sabotage it. Your agent, Poltavets, is a Russian mole and not the only one planted in your SBU."

"How do you know this?"

"I have a nephew with the SVR, like me he sees the madness in the Kremlin's actions in Ukraine. He gave me the Intel on Poltavets because he was part of the team running Poltavets."

"Was?"

"They changed his assignment when he questioned his superior."

Dudka wanted to spell it out. "You are telling me that the assassination of the investigative journalist – Anton Haymenko was a sanctioned operation conducted by the SVR, the Foreign Intelligence Service of the Russian Federation?"

"Yes, as much as anything the SVR does is sanctioned."

"Do you have details on other moles?"

"That's why I am here." Komarov reached into his cotton jacket and took out a padded A5 sized envelope, sunlight glinted on his wristwatch as he handed it to his old comrade.

Dudka took the envelope, the sun ignoring his own dull, steel watch. The envelope bore a Russian stamp, had been franked in Moscow and addressed to a 'Natalia Callas'. "Who is Miss Callas?"

"Mrs Callas is my daughter; she married a teacher. They live in Dubai."

"Congratulations."

"Thank you. In JVC."

"JVC?"

"Jumeriah Village Circle, it's an area of Dubai."

Dudka didn't care for the man's relative's living arrangements, "Why was this sent to her?"

"It was the safest way to get it out of Moscow."

"Hm." Dudka checked inside the envelope, it contained photographs and a USB stick. He carefully retrieved the photos, making sure that none of the other day trippers could see what they depicted. As he studied the images his mouth became dry. He reached for his beer and finished it.

"Do you recognise them?"

"I do." Dudka swallowed.

"Genna that is all you need to put a stop to this operation against the SBU."

"Thank you." Dudka cleared his throat, he needed a drink, something stronger than beer. "Vodka or Cognac?"

"Either, both."

Dudka pocketed the envelope, pushed up from his seat and

walked back along the aisle. He swayed slightly, was it the motion of the boat or was it him? He had worked some highly dangerous cases in his career, but the potential fallout from this could disable the service. He reached the bar on the lower deck.

The girl serving wore a tight top and a big smile. "What can I get you?"

Dudka forced his own face to smile, then squinted at the rows of bottles placed on wooden shelves affixed to the bulkhead. His eyes fell upon a half litre bottle of *Desna* cognac. "I'll take that, please." He paid, took his cognac and two disposable plastic cups back to his seat and sat.

"Desna? We are reliving old times." Komarov said.

Dudka opened the bottle, part filled the two cups and handed one to his colleague. "Did you know that 'Desna' means 'right hand' in Old Ruthenian?"

"I thought it was just a river?"

"That too," replied Dudka, "I hope that the right-hand knows what the left is doing."

Komarov frowned. "Meaning what?"

"You passing me this evidence risks your nephew's life."

"Do not look a gift horse in the mouth, Genna. Believe it or not, there are still some of us who view Ukraine warmly as our younger brother."

Ukraine was actually older than Russia, but Dudka let this pass. "Glad to hear it."

"My nephew wants to stop the violence. So do I."

"A noble sentiment."

Komarov raised his plastic cup. "Here's to noble sentiments!"

Dudka knocked back the cognac, it warmed him pleasantly. "We will need to question you."

"We?"

"Me."

Komarov seemed confused. "About what?"

"About the intelligence, you have given me."

"Ask me questions now, we have the time."

"Where did it come from?"

"I told you, it came directly from my nephew in Moscow."

"And he posted it to your daughter?"

"Yes, safer than sending it to me."

"Why did he send it now?"

"Because he has just been reassigned."

Dudka nodded. "Because he didn't agree with the operation against the SBU?"

"He didn't agree with the murder of Anton Haymenko."

"And he said this to his superiors?"

"Of course not."

"Why did your nephew - what's his name?"

"Sergey Savvin, my sister's boy."

"Why did Sergey give you this?"

"What was he supposed to do, go to a newspaper?" Komarov took the bottle and refilled both cups, the tremor in his hand had become more pronounced. "He knew I'd help him, and he knew I knew you."

"I see." Dudka decided to ease off on the questioning, for the moment. He raised his cup. "To your good health!"

"How is your daughter, by the way?" Komarov asked after swiftly emptying his cup.

"Fine. She has a very good job." Dudka didn't want to expand and certainly didn't want to mention that she too lived in Dubai. "And yours'?"

"She is doing very well. She loves the UAE and can you believe her daughter now is almost twelve?"

"Time flies."

"And your granddaughter is fifteen?"

"Yes."

Komarov poured more drinks. It was the third toast and traditionally this honoured women. "To our daughters and granddaughters!"

Both men drank, then lapsed into silence. Memories of Dudka's wife danced in his head as he watched the afternoon sun wink on the water, she would have been a proud grandmother.

"I have not been in Kyiv for a long time, I miss the place," Komarov said.

"Stay for a while, reacquaint yourself."

"I shall. I'm flying back on Wednesday."

"Where are you staying?"

"Some little place, near the centre."

"Call me if you want to meet."

Dudka poured the next shot; they nodded a mutual toast to each other before Komarov excused himself and headed for the lavatory. Dudka retrieved his iPhone and called Blazhevich. "Are you in position?"

"Yes, I'm on the boardwalk."

"Excellent." Dudka ended the call.

Komarov meandered back, his gait uneven. "This boat is unstable."

"And getting more so," Dudka said, as he emptied the remainder of the bottle equally into the plastic cups.

Zankovetskaya Street.

The sound of children playing in the square below drifted through the open kitchen window as did the odour of his neighbour's fried potatoes. Still feeling the effects of the cognac, Dudka fixed his weary eyes on the photographs and bank statements Blazhevich had printed from Komarov's USB stick. The young SBU agent butted the photos into two small piles. "Explain?"

"The images are from different sources, pile 'A' on the right are from an iPhone and 'B' are from stills from a digital surveillance camera at Haymenko's newspaper."

"The same surveillance camera whose footage, according to the building's Head of Security, had been corrupted," Dudka said, flatly. "Pay him a friendly visit, what's his name?"

"Ruslan Fedorov."

Dudka plucked the top photograph from pile 'B'. It showed a figure standing in an underground car park holding a mobile phone. Eyes narrowing, he took in the suspect's angular nose and sharp chin. "Can you confirm the suspect in this photograph is Director Zlotnik?"

"Yes," Blazhevich understood the gravity of the question. "But I can't confirm that it's a single photograph."

Dudka's brow furrowed. "It's what, a collage?"

"Potentially, it's a lower resolution image - harder to be definitive."

Dudka pawed the next photo from pile 'B'. It showed Zlotnik

standing in the same place but now joined by Senior Agents Poltavets and Leskov; two men he had directly promoted and transferred from Donetsk. "And the same for this one?"

"Yes."

Dudka nodded slowly, he now took a photo from pile 'A', the most incriminating image allegedly showed Poltavets tampering with Haymenko's car. Dudka placed it side by side on the tabletop with the previous images. "These were taken in the same place within minutes of each other, but Poltavets' photo is sharper, taken with the iPhone?"

"Yes."

"When?"

"I wrote it on the back," Blazhevich turned the print over. "10:28 on the 17th of December."

"An hour before the assassination."

"The GPS coordinates are the same as Haymenko's office car park."

Dudka flicked through pile 'A'. There were photos of Poltavets by Haymenko's car and photos of Poltavets and Leskov together with Haymenko's car in the background; there was also one of Zlotnik. He stood in the car park with the two men, but Haymenko's car was not in the background. Dudka turned over the print. It was taken three hours after the others. "So Zlotnik was there on the same day but later?"

"Yes."

Dudka closed his eyes and tried to recollect his actions six months before. "The explosion happened outside the building. I didn't see Zlotnik at the scene and he didn't tell me he had been there."

"I can't remember him there either."

"But they were." Dudka tapped the photo. "I drafted them in to help." Dudka re-examined the pile 'B' photo of the three men. It was a similar shot, but a different angle and resolution. "Vitaly, we must take Poltavets and Leskov into custody but any action against them will alert Zlotnik. And as yet we don't know how he is connected with this, if at all." Dudka jutted his chin at the pile of bank statements. "If that account is real and the statement is genuine, we shall have proof positive."

Blazhevich swallowed. "Why did Komarov suddenly give you this intelligence?"

"His nephew has just sent it to him."

"By post?"

"By post."

"That's not secure."

"It arrived."

"The assassination was six months ago; the timing feels odd."

"Or perfect, the case is cold, and we are being pushed by Zlotnik for results."

"Is Zlotnik a mole?"

"He's a bumptious fool, but a traitor? Two piles of prints, 'A' are genuine and 'B' may not be? But if one allegation is false the other may also be." Dudka suddenly smiled and pointed at Blazhevich. "Trojan Horse."

"Sorry?"

"Komarov said 'don't look a gift horse in the mouth' but is this a gift horse, what if it's a 'Trojan Horse'? Are Poltavets and Leskov being sacrificed to mislead us?"

Blazhevich followed Dudka's train of thought. "To make us

willing to suspect Zlotnik of being an SVR mole?"

"Exactly. The Russians want us chasing shadows, questioning agency integrity. Either way, this will eat up directorate man hours."

Blazhevich's phone beeped. He glanced at Dudka who nodded his consent before he checked his email. "It's the list of the hotel guests from Dubai."

Dudka held out his hand. "Let me see."

"You just move your fingers like this," Blazhevich did so, "to make the image larger."

This much Dudka did know, but he nodded and took the iPhone. He squinted at the display and read the names, one he recognised. "Sergey Savvin."

Premier Palace Hotel, Kyiv

'Little place, my foot', Dudka murmured as he crossed the impressive marble lobby and joined a queue of elderly tourists at the check-in desk. The Premier Palace was one of the new hotels that had appeared in the last decade to charge inflated Western prices for Western standards of service. The guests in line he pegged to be Canadian Ukrainian diaspora, based upon the red maple leaf badges pinned to their jackets. They were returning to the lands of their ancestors, Dudka hoped they had adequate travel insurance.

"Good afternoon, sir," the receptionist automatically spoke in English. "Are you with the 'Kyiv History Tour' group?"

Dudka brandished his SBU ID card. "I need to check your security tapes."

Her smile remained but her brow wrinkled as she processed the query. "Our Security Manager, Mr Makarenko is the only person who could permit such a request. I shall call him."

Dudka was met several minutes later by Makarenko, a hefty gentleman wearing a suit too short in the leg. Makarenko led him into his office. On a desk a large flat-screen monitor showed the feed from numerous surveillance cameras. Makarenko angled it away. "Please take a seat."

Dudka did. "I need to examine your footage from the last three days."

"Such a request needs to be made in writing." Makarenko smiled, without sincerity.

Dudka produced a pen. "Do you have a piece of paper?"

"That's not what I meant."

"I know." Dudka sighed. In the days of the KGB, a refusal meant at best arrest and at worse a mystery tour of the salt mines. "Listen to me, Makarenko. I'm a director of the SBU and I am requesting to review your tapes. I'm sure such an honourable establishment as this has nothing to hide?"

Makarenko's left eye twitched. "Of course. I'll show you how to operate the system."

Dudka found the instructions relatively easy to follow, which he presumed they had to be for an ape, like Makarenko, to understand. "Thank you. You may go now."

"Regulations state I must be present in the room."

Dudka glowered at the man who was double his weight and half his age. "Go."

Once alone Dudka selected the recording of the lobby footage and typed in a time stamp for Saturday morning. He ran the footage forward at varying speeds, guests glided across the screen and then Oleg Komarov appeared. He approached the check-in desk. Dudka watched his old colleague step away from the desk and towards the lifts. A man in a dark suit intercepted him. Komarov stiffened as though surprised. The pair took a table in the lobby bar, on the very edge of the camera's field of vision. Dudka watched the conversation for its five-minute entirety and saw the man hand an envelope to Komarov, a padded envelope. Dudka squinted at the screen; he needed a clearer image. Pausing playback, he left the office to find Makarenko. He was along the corridor chatting to a woman wearing a maid's uniform, at least he imagined she was a maid. "I need to zoom in on the screen and make prints."

An hour later Dudka sat at his desk, sipping black tea. He handed Blazhevich a copy of the digital surveillance tape and a thin pile of printed screenshots. "Use your magic computers to find out who this is. I've a hunch it's Sergey Savvin."

Blazhevich looked surprised. "This is odd."

"How?"

Blazhevich opened his case notes and scanned the information he'd received from Atlantis, Dubai. He found what he wanted, enlarged it on his screen then turned the tablet around. "In addition to the guest list from the hotel, a contact of mine at UAE immigration sent me scanned images of the corresponding passports. This one looked familiar to me."

Dudka peered at the screen, it looked to him like the same man who had met Komarov at the hotel. "Savvin?"

"But he also looks exactly like the Head of Security at Haymenko's newspaper, Ruslan Fedorov!"

"He doctored the footage?" Dudka asked, an answer already forming in his mind.

"I've got an idea." Blazhevich tapped away at his tablet. "I'm accessing immigration records. Got it!" On the screen a passport with a remarkably similar looking photograph to Savvin's but issued under the name 'Ruslan Fedorov' displayed. "In the last year he's made trips to both Dubai and Russia. According to immigration he is currently in Ukraine."

Sviatoshyn district, Kyiv

Dudka wore a cardigan under his suit jacket to combat the predawn chill seeping in through the part-open window of his ancient Volga. He was parked up at the side of Victory Avenue. The six-lane artery, empty save for grumbling, belching trucks, would later be thick with commuters. He'd been stationary for an hour, keeping watch on the target address. The building was on the corner of Victory Avenue and Zhyvopysna Street, their suspect's flat was on the eighteenth floor. Dudka watched the front of the building whilst a four-man team from the SBU's elite counter-terrorist ALPHA unit waited in a VW Transporter covering the rear. Dudka checked his iPhone. It read 04:57. In three minutes three teams would assault three different targets. He would handle the arrest of Ruslan Fedorov, eighteen floors above; three miles away Blazhevich and his team would take Poltavets into custody whilst the third, led by the Head of the ALPHA unit, would take Leskov. Dudka pressed the transmit button on his radio and gave his ALPHA assault team the 'go' command. As five a.m. arrived an SBU technician flicked a switch and all mobile communication for the local area ceased. The ALPHA's broke cover and snaked out of their van. Splitting into two groups, they entered the building from both entrances at once, quickly clearing the deserted foyer before taking the stairs up to the eighteenth floor. Dudka stepped out of the Passat and slipped on a dark blue SBU flak jacket before he entered the building. Via the secure comms net, Dudka listened as the team leader confirmed he was on the eighteenth floor. Less than a minute later there was a dull thud as a shaped charge blew open the front door and the commandos gained entry to the flat. The next sound Dudka heard was the team leader confirming that they had secured Fedorov.

Dudka rode the lift to the eighteenth floor. One commando saluted him on the landing whilst another nodded as he stepped through what remained of Fedorov's front door and into his hall. Immediately ahead Dudka saw their target kneeling in the middle of the living room, with his hands plasticuffed behind his back, naked apart from a pair of greying boxer shorts. The last two ALPHA members stood by his side, cradling their machine pistols, reminding Dudka of big game hunters posing for glory.

Fedorov glowered, "Who do you think you are? You've got nothing on me!"

"I'm sure that's not true," Dudka said, with a smile. "Put him in the van."

"Wait! I don't know who you think I am, but you're wrong!" Fedorov pleaded, loudly as he was roughly pulled to his feet. "You can't do this! I've got diplomatic immunity!"

"How?" Dudka scowled. "Tell me?"

"I'll show you. My passport is in the top drawer of that unit." Fedorov's bobbed his head to the left.

The nearest commando placed his hand on the drawer. "Let me, sir."

Dudka sensed something, he saw Fedorov shut his eyes, he saw Fedorov flinch. "Stop!" Dudka roared. But he was too late.

Dudka registered a flash but not the thunderous noise that a millisecond later followed it. The shockwave lifted Dudka from his feet and hurled him back out into the communal landing. He hit the lift doors and then darkness hit him.

Zankovetskaya Street, Kyiv

Dudka opened his front door and regarded his visitor. "Yuri Ruslanovich, if you're trying to sell me something I'm not interested."

Yuri Ruslanovich Zlotnik raised his left hand, it held a bottle of vodka. "Amusing as always, Genna."

"Come in." Dudka waited whilst his boss removed his shoes, then led him slowly towards the living room. Classical music, a concert, drifted from the television. Dudka turned it off and sat in an armchair.

"Are you allowed to drink yet?"

"I am."

"Then this is for you." Zlotnik placed the vodka on Dudka's coffee table and sat opposite him.

"Thank you."

"How are you feeling?"

Dudka didn't reply. He'd had a concussion, numerous lacerations and a week after the explosion still ached all over but this was nothing; his heart bled for the families of the two dead ALPHA commandos.

Zlotnik's nose twitched. "Is that borsch I can smell?"

"Yes," Dudka nodded and wished he hadn't as a sharp pain travelled up his neck. "It's Saturday."

Zlotnik eyed the vodka but when Dudka made no move to open it, he spoke. "Gennady Stepanovich this is not an easy thing for me to admit but I was wrong about Poltavets and Leskov."

"You were," Dudka replied flatly.

"I want to thank you for exonerating me."

"I just stated the facts."

"Your investigation was most thorough."

"That was mostly Blazhevich."

Immediately after the explosion Blazhevich had taken over the responsibility for the investigation. Poltavets had refused to make a statement, but Leskov had. His statement detailed his and Poltavets involvement with the now deceased Sergey Savvin. Leskov had made it clear that Zlotnik had never been a part of the operation. But Blazhevich had kept digging, specifically looking at Zlotnik's offshore bank account and payments into it from Russia. Zlotnik eventually confirmed that these related to a property investment, which although legal should have been declared. Blazhevich, on Dudka's say so had contracted selective amnesia and failed to add this to the report, which had now been rubber stamped by the National Security and Defence Council.

Zlotnik eyed the bottle again. "Can we drink?"

"If you insist." Dudka removed two shot glasses from a drawer under the tabletop, opened the bottle and poured.

Zlotnik held up his glass. "To you, Gennady Stepanovich."

"To me." It was tepid and tasteless, Dudka managed to hide his displeasure both at the vodka and the presence of his guest.

"I had a meeting with the President today."

"And how is Volodymyr Oleksandrovych?"

A momentary flash of annoyance crossed Zlotnik's face before he replied, it irked him that Dudka personally knew the President of Ukraine. "He is satisfied that the Haymenko case is closed, however, he is aware of the unfavourable publicity for the SBU."

"I am sure you will be able to mitigate any such bad PR." Dudka poured more vodka. "To you, Yuri Ruslanovich."

Zlotnik drained his glass. "You are the longest-serving SBU Director in the history of the SBU."

"A fact you've previously reminded me of."

"Indeed. You have countless achievements within the service. At your time of life many, indeed most think about how best to enjoy the rest of the time they have. Would it not be best when you leave the service to end on a high note?"

"I don't sing."

Zlotnik ignored the comment and continued. "You were not responsible for the deaths of our two men, Genna but were wounded whilst successfully countering an SVR operation. You could retire now, as a hero with your reputation intact and your career celebrated."

Dudka folded his arms. "You want me to retire?"

"Want is too harsh a word, but retirement may well be the best course of action."

Dudka had thought about this, about the two men he'd lost. "Best for who, you?"

"Now Genna, we knew that one day this would happen."

"That you would feel so threatened by me that you deem it necessary for me to resign?"

"Retire, with full honours."

"If I retired and left you running the service, I would have no honour."

"You were blown up!" Zlotnik sat back in the chair, frustrated. "Is this how it will always be? I try my best with you, I really do Genna but there is always this unresolved anger you have."

Dudka raised his eyebrows, genuinely surprised. "There is no anger, I just want what is best for our nation."

"And that is not me?"

"Don't be paranoid."

"I am not!" Zlotnik snapped back, his voice louder than he had intended.

"I think we should have another drink." Dudka again poured. "The investigation is complete, and you have been exonerated. Be happy. We have both had to deal with a lot of stress. Perhaps you should take a holiday? I hear Dubai is nice."

Zlotnik's eyes narrowed, but he said nothing.

Boryspil International Airport, Kyiv

Dudka hadn't been in the business lounge before and wasn't overly impressed with what he saw. The room was open plan and decorated in grey tones which matched the overcast sky. An open bar top took up part of one wall and at random intervals, faux leather armchairs and settees clustered around uncomfortably low coffee tables. By one of these sat Oleg Komarov, his table covered with empty glasses and a plate of pastries. His didn't see Dudka until he was all but sitting opposite him.

"Genna? Why are you here?" Komarov slurred.

Dudka folded his arms. "Your flight is delayed."

Komarov peered at the nearest departures screen. "It is?"

"And it will only leave when I am happy with what you tell me."

"Hasn't the SBU done enough already to ruin me? They held me for three days and your boy Blazhevich questioned me for a whole day before he let me go." Komarov's shoulders slumped, he reached for his glass and gulped the free whisky.

"Fine, go ahead."

Dudka glanced around, his neck complained, the lounge was almost empty with no one near enough to overhear them. "I'm sorry about Savvin."

Komarov's eyebrows shot skywards. "You are sorry? It was him who tried to blow you up."

"I'm sorry he's dead."

"I'm not. He threatened my family."

"I know." Dudka looked at a pastry on Komarov's plate. He was tempted. "Why did you play me for a fool Oleg?"

"Play you? I gave you credible intelligence on Russian moles within the SBU."

"You gave me credible intelligence on two moles, and incredible intelligence on the Head of the SBU."

"I had no idea."

"We are both too old for fairy tales, Oleg."

"Genna, I studied the intelligence, I saw nothing wrong with it. All this I explained to Agent Blazhevich!"

"You lied to me about how you came by the intelligence."

"I told you who gave it to me."

Yes, you did but Savvin did not send it to you. I watched surveillance footage of Savvin handing you an envelope on Saturday afternoon at your hotel."

"Yes." Komarov drank again.

"And you gave me that same envelope."

"I did, he insisted upon it."

"All part of his narrative."

"You saw, Genna, he put my daughter's address on the envelope. It was a threat."

"Did he give you my home telephone number?" This had worried Dudka.

"Yes."

"And he paid you?"

"You know he did." Komarov looked down, fiddled with his expensive wristwatch.

"Did you know he was the bomb maker?"

"No. If I had known that I would have not let any of this happen. You must believe me Genna."

"I must."

Komarov drank again, became belligerent. "So, what are you going to do now Genna, arrest me again?"

"What purpose would it serve? Revenge? You were just the messenger."

"I was! That is all I was."

"Whilst I've been convalescing, I've been thinking, a lot. Savvin chose you believing our connection would make me less vigorous in examining the evidence. He took a gamble that a pair of old goats would be easier to fool than someone younger. And by giving up two real SVR assets his intelligence was all the more credible."

"That's exactly it Genna. I wanted to help you, and I wanted my family to be safe."

Dudka succumbed to a pastry and chewed it as a Ukrainian International Airlines jet taxied past the window. "Savvin is an ambitious SVR officer, he wants to make a name for himself. So, what does he do? He formulates a plan to destabilise the SBU, to have us searching everywhere for traitors, to make us seem utterly corrupt by having me investigate Director Zlotnik. But that is not all."

"No?" Komarov leant forward.

"No. He wants to show that he did indeed know more than his boss – the man in charge of the operation against the SBU." Dudka brushed a crumb from his tie. "By leaking the identity of two agents, he wanted to show that the operation was ill planned. He'd probably written a report, backdated, to say as much. He wants his boss' job."

"So, this was all for his career?"

"Yes." Dudka sighed. "He failed in that but what he achieved is far bigger than that. When Zlotnik and I publicly announce that a Russian agent was responsible for the assassination of Anton Haymenko, some quarters will believe me and others, cheered on by Russia, will scream that the SBU was culpable all along."

"I'm sorry."

"What for? You were just the messenger." Dudka stood. "You can go back to sunny Dubai now, Oleg."

"Thank you, Genna." Komarov pulled himself out of his seat and extended his hand, but Dudka was already walking away.

AUTHOR BIOGRAPHY

Alex Shaw is the author of three international bestselling thriller series featuring Aidan Snow, Jack Tate, and Sophie

Racine, and the standalone, *Delta Force Vampire*. His writing has also been published in several thriller anthologies. *Total Blackout*, the first in his Jack Tate series, was Shortlisted for the 2021 Wilbur Smith Adventure Writing prize – Best Published Novel. Alex is commercially published by HQ Harper Collins in English and Luzifer Verlag in German. He is an active member of The International Thriller Writers' organisation and the CWA.

Alex, his wife and their two sons divide their time between homes in Kyiv - Ukraine, Sussex - England and Dubai. Follow Alex on twitter: @alexshawhetman or Instagram @alexshawthrillerwriter or BookBub @AlexShaw or find him on Facebook. Alex is represented by Justin Nash of The Kate Nash Literary Agency. @JustinNashLit

The Writers

by Annabel Kantaria

◆◆◆◆

Bethany's already eating breakfast in the hotel's airy restaurant when she sees Alia hesitate at the door, eyes scanning the tables. The place is humming, but the service is efficient, and Bethany had hoped to be finished long before Alia appeared. She flicks her eyes back to her phone and pretends not to have seen her. But no such luck.

'Hey!' Alia slides into the seat across the table from her without waiting to be invited. With her comes a waft of her sickly perfume that takes Bethany right back to their teenage years – in a bad way.

'Hey.' Beth can barely break a smile. Hasn't she already made it obvious that she'd rather be alone than with Alia? How many clues did the woman need?

'Morning!' Alia says. 'I'm gonna grab a coffee.' She waves at a waiter. 'Want anything?'

Beth points with her eyes to the bagel and cream cheese already on her plate and shakes her head.

'Just a coffee,' Alia tells the waiter. When it comes, she holds the cup in both hands and blows on it: another of her habits that disgusts Bethany. She shifts her plate slightly further away from the reach of Alia's breath.

'Last day!' Alia sings, as if they're best friends enjoying a frivolous mini break. 'We've got till about six before we need to leave for the airport. What d'you wanna do? Shopping? Sight-seeing? It's a beautiful day.'

Bethany sighs and checks her phone, not caring if her scowl is obvious. She snorts a little air out through her nose, clicks the phone screen off and puts it back down, wishing Alia would get it through her thick head that, for Bethany, this is not a sight-seeing trip. It is a work trip. And, furthermore, it's looking like she's going to have to chalk it up as a very expensive work trip that's yielded no results, aka a complete waste of time and money.

'Honestly? I haven't even thought about it,' Bethany says. 'I was hoping to have heard from at least one of the agents while I was here, so we could have a face-to-face meeting while I'm still in the country.'

Alia pulls a sympathetic face and stirs her coffee, the spoon jangling too loudly against the china.

'God, they have no idea what we've gone through to be here!' Bethany says, and it comes out harsher than she intended as the week's frustration roils within her. 'It's such a big deal when you live in Dubai! It's not like we've "nipped" down from San Francisco.' She clicks her tongue against her teeth and tries to calm herself. 'I guess you can't rush these things. As with everything, they'll get in touch in their own sweet time.' She sighs again.

'Well, for what it's worth, I'm glad I came,' Alia says. 'It's been great to see L.A.'

'I guess,' Beth agrees, annoyed that Alia is being more philosophical than she is. 'It's good experience to pitch to those guys, and hopefully something will come of it further down the line.'

'You haven't heard from anyone yet?' Alia asks.

'Well, I got a "no" from that Teresa woman but that's okay. It wasn't for her, anyway, really. And a "no" from David, too. But he was weird, right? I'm sure he was off his head on something. I just pitched to them for the experience – I knew they wouldn't take it. The one I'm really hoping for is Amber Solio. She's the perfect agent for me. I really like her, and my script is right up her street. We've been chatting on socials, and we got on so well in person. We were on the same page. I can see us building a great relationship, and she said she loved my pitch – so, yeah. Fingers crossed.'

Alia nods. 'Yeah, fingers crossed.' She pauses. 'And maybe if you don't get any leads from this it's time to re-think. I mean, maybe there's something to learn from the feedback.'

'Hmm,' Bethany says.

'I heard from Amber,' Alia adds, as if it's an after-thought.

'You what?' Bethany's head snaps up.

'Amber phoned.'

'When?' Bethany can't breathe. This can't be happening. Her instinct is to check her phone. Has she missed a call herself?

'Yesterday. About six o'clock.'

'Why didn't you say?' But Bethany knows the answer – she'd blocked Alia's suggestion that they go out for dinner together and had met up with an old university friend in Beverly Hills instead.

'I didn't see you after it happened.' Alia shrugs one shoulder dismissively.

'So, what did she say?' The words squeeze out through the tightness in Bethany's throat. Under the table, her hands clench into fists. 'Do you think she's calling everyone?'

'Hmm. Not sure. She said I'm naturally talented.' Alia puffs up as she says it. Bethany's heart thuds behind her ribs.

'She likes my idea, she thinks I "have something", and she believes I can do it.' Alia twirls a strand of hair around her finger and sucks her cheeks. 'It's so nice to have that validation. You know, I'm beginning to think that this is my thing. That I was born to tell my story. I mean, people love my captions on Instagram.'

Bethany sits back in the booth and tries to regulate her breathing before she speaks. She can't believe what she's hearing. Writing has been *her* dream since school; never Alia's. All Alia ever wanted was to be an influencer.

'She knows it's a rom-com, doesn't she?' Bethany says tightly. 'I thought she hated romance.'

'I know, right?' Alia laughs and tosses her hair over her shoulder releasing another wave of that nausea-inducing perfume. 'Even I didn't think I'd get a call-back from her. But – yeah – she said she couldn't stop thinking about the pitch. She asked to see the script!'

Beth relaxes a fraction, a glimmer of glee sparking inside her. Alia doesn't have a script. She hasn't written a script in her life.

'So, what will you do?' Bethany asks with *faux* innocence. 'I mean, you haven't actually got anything to show her, have you?'

Alia pulls an awkward face.

'Well, I *didn't* have anything to show her,' she says with a smile. 'But I had nothing else to do last night when you were out, so I started to write it. I mean, I have an idea of what I want to do with it, so I wrote the opening pages and sent them over to her late last night to show her what I had in mind and, yeah, so...'

Alia's voice peters out into an awkward silence. She takes a sip of her coffee. Bethany smears cream cheese on the last side of her bagel and takes a bite as she tries to calm her breathing.

'So that's it?' Bethany asks after she's swallowed that mouthful. 'You left it like that?' On the table, her hands roll up a paper napkin and twist it into a snake, tighter and tighter, until it starts to buckle in on itself. Maybe Alia will never finish the script. It's one thing to begin one, all creative and fired up, but quite another to work it through to a satisfying end. Writing a screenplay is a little more demanding than writing Instagram captions – as the Master of Fine Arts certificate hanging on Bethany's office wall would concur.

'Well, she sent a WhatsApp this morning to say she liked what I'd written, so, who knows, eh?'

Bethany shoves the ruined paper napkin away. 'Really?'

Alia's phone rings. She stares at it, her hand over her mouth.

'It's her,' she says. 'Oh my god.' She flicks back her hair, clicks on the call and says, 'Good morning. Alia Rawad speaking,' as if she's the president of a FTSE 500 company. Then she gets up and walks over to the patio doors that lead to the pool area to take the call.

The bagel Bethany eats sticks in her mouth in a claggy, dry lump. She wonders if she can leave now before Alia comes back with whatever news it is that's making her nod and smile and throw her head back to laugh on the phone with Amber Solio, but Bethany isn't quick enough. Already, Alia's walking back towards her, flushed and smiling.

'Okay,' she says, all cheerful as she slips back into her seat, 'so that was Amber. Obviously! She loved the pages I sent, so we had a chat, and she loves that I have a platform and, long story short, she's...' Alia beats a drum-roll on the table with her hands... 'preparing a contract!'

'What?' The word shoots out of Bethany's mouth along with a

small piece of chewed bagel, which she wipes from the table with the twisted napkin.

'Yeah! She wants me to go into the offices at ten to sign it! Isn't that amazing?' Alia beams at Bethany then looks at her watch. 'I guess I'll have to get an Uber.'

Beth is shaking her head. 'She wants to sign you? Without seeing a full script?' She stares accusingly at Alia. 'Agents never do that.'

Alia shrugs and sips her coffee, like she'll wait for Bethany to figure out herself that literary agents clearly do do that.

'Anyway,' Alia continues after the silence stretches a little too far. 'She said she has agency writers who can help me out, if I get stuck. But she thinks my story has an important message and she wants to get it made. She said it's a refreshing change to the usual "boring thrillers". So now I've just got to write it as quickly as I can.' She laughs. 'That'll be fun! Might have to take a little sabbatical from work. Eek.'

'Wow,' Bethany says, looking at Alia through narrowed eyes. 'Really wow. That's amazing.'

'Thanks,' Alia says. 'So, yeah, looping back to what we said earlier: I'm so glad I came! It's been totally worth it!' She notices Bethany's face and changes her tone. 'I could put in a good word for you if you like? Tell her that you're a really good writer. Does she know you've already published a book?'

'It was on my pitch.' Bethany's smile is small and tight. There's a tell-tale wobble at the corners of her mouth and she realises she's close to tears. 'Well,' she says, trying to pull herself together. 'It sounds like you won't have time for much sight-seeing, what with your meeting and everything, so don't worry about me. I'll do my own thing and you do you.'

'Whatever you want,' Alia says. 'I'll see if you're here but, if you're not, I'll come by your room just before six?'

'Sure. Right, gonna pack.' Bethany stands. 'See ya.'

Back in her room, Bethany throws herself onto her unmade bed and punches the pillow as hard as she can. This is so unfair. She's the one who did the research, who found the best pitch conference in Los Angeles, and planned the trip. Alia would never have thought of it herself if Rania hadn't put her big, stupid foot in it and bragged that Bethany was flying to L.A. to pitch a film script to top agents, managers and producers.

Alia's never wanted to be a scriptwriter. It hasn't been *her* dream since she was a child. Bethany's the one with the beautifully crafted crime thriller to sell, not Alia with her schmaltzy little notion of a rom-com. For Alia, this is just a fad – something she fancied having a go at because she couldn't bear for Bethany to achieve success of her own. It's a pattern that Bethany's seen repeat over and over since they were kids.

Bethany realises that her heart's racing with the anger coursing through her. She presses her hand to her chest and feels the thump. She gets up and paces the room breathing deeply: six steps towards the window, six steps back, skirting around the bed as her mind spirals. What if Alia actually manages to finish the script? What if the movie gets made? What if it's really successful? Wins awards? What if Alia gets invited to Cannes or wins a frickin' Oscar?

Bethany realises she's getting ahead of herself. She goes to the window and tries to calm herself down. How could Alia's film have any substance, she asks herself? Alia's never studied writing, doesn't know anything about structure, conflict or rising action; wouldn't recognise a smoking gun if it was pointed right at her.

Yes, Bethany tells herself as she stares out at the glorious colours of Palisades Park and the glittering ocean beyond. Alia's script will be rubbish. She might be signing with an agent, but it'll probably all come to nothing. Surely, this will all pass?

She gets herself ready for the day, then checks her phone one more time and her breath catches. There, in her inbox is an email from Amber Solio. Bethany sits on the bed and takes a deep breath before she opens it with shaking hands. Maybe they'll both sign with the Solio Agency. That would *just about* make things all right.

Dear Bethany,

Thanks for pitching on Tuesday. It was great to meet you.

I liked your idea very much, and your pitch was both solid and commercial. However, I'm only able to dedicate time to one new client at the present time and the competition was fierce, so I'm going to pass for now.

Wishing you all the best for the future,

Amber Solio

Bethany can't breathe. This is it: the end of the road she's travelled for so long, and it's a brick wall. She's been thinking only positive thoughts since the day she first read about the pitch festival. Her idea is both unique and high concept. Her treatment is original. Her pitch is strong. She's friends with Amber on Twitter, where she engages with her not only about her new kitten and but also her hideous knitting hobby. She's done everything she can to manifest a 'yes' from Amber Solio and she's never let herself believe that she might not get one. She's saved her money and sacrificed her holiday leave to fly to L.A. but now the rejection is there in black and white.

She clicks the 'X' and puts her phone down, then remains seated, her fingernails drumming an insistent rhythm on the bedside table to her right, as she stares out of the window, her mind racing. There is absolutely no way she's going to spend the day sightseeing and pretending to be happy for Alia. No way, José.

She has a far better idea.

She waits until she sees Alia climb into a cab on the street below, then she calls an Uber and leaves the hotel herself.

It's 5.55pm when Alia knocks on Bethany's door. Alia's dressed in the overpriced travel co-ord she was gifted in return for promoting the brand, and is dragging her suitcase behind her.

'Hey, how was your day?' Alia asks. 'Sorry I didn't call sooner. I was out all day then I started writing because – you know! I kind of have to!'

Bethany feels that like a punch to her gut. 'It was good, thanks. How about you?' She can't bear to ask about the meeting with Amber.

'Oh great! Amber gave me a tour of the offices, which are *so* cool, so I got to meet all the other agents at Solio, then we signed the contract, and Amber took me out to this really edgy café to celebrate – so nice of her, as she's actually, like, *so* busy. Then I came back to Santa Monica and went to this awesome Farmer's Market on Main Street that Amber told me about. I took in some art galleries and stuff, then went to the pier because it's so iconic. I've always wanted to go there. So, yeah, all in, a brilliant day.'

'Sounds great,' Bethany says.

'Anyway, look, I don't want to rush you, but we really ought to get going. I've looked at the traffic and it's gonna take a while to get to the airport. Amber said to leave loads of time because security at LAX can take ages.'

'Sure,' Bethany says, recoiling at the way Alia drops Amber into the conversation like she's her new best friend. 'I'm almost ready. But I'll be a couple more minutes so why don't you come in?'

On the bed, Bethany's suitcase is closed and, next to it, sits a bulky washbag.

'I just can't fit this in,' Bethany says. 'I don't have an inch of space. I'd put it in my hand luggage, but I can't take liquids on board, right? Such a shame. I'll have to leave some stuff behind, but I don't know what because I use it all.' She looks sadly at the washbag. 'Sit down. I need to unpack a bit while I figure it out.'

Alia looks at the washbag then at her watch. 'I have room,' she says.

Bethany stops rummaging. 'What? In your bag?'

'Yeah. I always travel quite light. I'm sure it'll fit. It's just this, right? Nothing else?'

'Yeah, just that. Really?' A huge smile lights up Bethany's face. 'That would be amazing. Thank you. Then I'm ready.'

Alia squats down and opens her bag on the floor. 'Here, pass it over.' She rummages about in her things, adds the washbag, then closes the lid of her bag, zips it up and locks it.

'Done. Right, let's get going. We don't want to miss this flight.'

'Ready!' Beth says. She takes one more glance around the room, then the two of them roll their luggage towards the lifts.

By the time the plane lands in Dubai, Bethany and Alia have been on it for over fifteen hours. Neither of them has had much sleep: Alia because she's been typing away on her laptop, and Bethany because every tap of Alia's fingers on the keyboard winds her up a little more.

'Ready?' Alia asks as the queue to exit the plane begins to shuffle forward. 'Got everything?'

'Yep. You?' Bethany says.

Alia taps her bag with a smile. 'The most important thing is in here. I've finished Act One already.' Her eyes are shining – she looks rejuvenated, not like she's just had a sleepless night hurtling through the night in a metal tube.

'Great.' Bethany can't be bothered to sound more enthusiastic.

The two of them make their way through the e-gates at passport control and, as they enter the baggage reclaim area, Bethany winces and rubs her stomach.

'Ooh. Ow. I think I must have eaten something... I need the bathroom. Badly. Shit! You go ahead. You must be exhausted.'

Alia's eyes flick to the carousel where the bags are already coming out.

'I can wait, it's okay.'

'No, it's fine. Really. I don't know how long I'll be.' She grimaces. 'You get going.'

Alia shrugs. 'Okay. If, you're sure. My driver's already here, so I probably should.'

Beth waits a few minutes in the bathroom. When she emerges, her bag's circulating on the conveyor. She scans the Arrivals Hall and spots Alia up ahead, her ponytail swinging from side to side as she strides towards Customs. Bethany retrieves her bag and follows at a discrete distance, entering Customs close enough to see Alia's jolt of surprise as two grim-faced, uniformed officers step forward to intercept her. She feels Alia's confusion as she's led firmly towards an interview room, but Alia is still smiling politely and nodding. She knows that all baggage is scanned on arrival in Dubai, but she has nothing to hide.

As the door swings closed behind them, Bethany knows Alia will be telling the Customs officers there must be some kind of mistake – that she's a good person, she's never taken drugs in her life. She'll say that maybe someone accidentally dropped something on her bag at LAX but that it's nothing to do with her. She'll be telling them they're welcome to search her luggage and she'll be one hundred per cent sure that they'll find nothing untoward inside it – until she remembers, perhaps, the washbag she offered to carry for Bethany.

Maybe that'll be the moment she realises that you can't treat people the way she's treated Bethany since they were ten years old. That you can't walk all over your friends, belittle them and use them. That you can't invite yourself into their careers, steal their agents and trample on their dreams. Maybe that's when she'll realise that writers of "the usual boring thrillers" can think up brilliant revenge plots.

Beth smiles to herself as she walks unhindered through Customs to the taxi queue. It had been so easy to get the drugs in Venice Beach; child's play to get Alia to carry them. And, with the amount of heroin she's planted in that washbag, Alia won't be in any position to get her script out for the best part of the next decade. As Bethany slips into a waiting cab, she opens her emails and starts typing, 'Dear Amber… I'm so sorry to have to tell you…'

Maybe the trip would be worth it, after all.

AUTHOR BIOGRAPHY

Annabel Kantaria won the inaugural Montegrappa Writing Prize at the Emirates Airline Festival of Literature and has gone on to publish five psychological thrillers with HQ Stories at Harper Collins UK, under her own name and the pseudonym Anna Kent. A sixth is underway. Annabel is the resident writing mentor for the Emirates Literature Foundation Seddiqi Writers' Fellowship in the UAE. She also works as an editorial coach, teaches workshops on writing and editing, and speaks and moderates at various literary festivals around the world. For further information, visit: www.annabelkantaria.com.

Say My Name

by Gal Podjarny

◆◆◆◆

Despite her previous apprehension, she left the office building feeling buoyant. The job interview had gone better than she'd expected. The people she'd met were friendly and respectful, plus each one was from a different ethnicity, as if the company was collecting. She had a conversation with a woman named Wanangwa about getting white people to pronounce your name properly.

"It's pronounced like at the end of loch if you were Scottish: mee-x-al," Michal had said to Wanangwa, remembering endless phone calls. Talking to surgery receptionists was particularly vexing, like rolling a rock up a hill. She never got the same one on the line and they never understood what she wanted from them.

"No, there's no nickname you can use," Wanangwa said, laughing.

"I particularly love it when they say it's an exotic name. I had three other Michals in my class growing up."

Wanangwa had nodded emphatically, and Michal felt understood for the first time in a long while. She walked down the block, still analysing that conversation, when something caught her eye. She did a double take.

It was herself... *on the other side of the street.*

She blinked, her brain processing her doppelganger. She wore the same navy skirt suit and black high heels, her hair the same curly onyx black. She had seen pictures of herself from the side, and this woman had the exact same profile. Without really having a plan, she started toward the other woman.

The doppelganger kept walking as if she hadn't seen Michal. Michal was sure that had she seen her, she would have stopped and stared. This was too weird to just let go. She had to figure out what was happening.

Michal followed the woman to the tube and got on after her. She had an odd feeling, like being jet lagged. Her brain felt too liquid to focus. She spent the whole ride playing a future conversation between her and the doppelganger in her head. But she couldn't bring herself to approach the woman now advancing down the carriage to find a seat. Her feet had frozen into their place. Michal couldn't take her eyes off the woman, who was too busy with her phone to look up. The similarities were uncanny. It wasn't like identical twins, who look similar but have, especially in their early forties, distinguishing markers. This was like looking in the mirror.

The doppelganger stepped off the train. Michal followed her without thinking. She only realised it was also her stop after they'd left the station. Her lower belly started feeling heavy, but she dismissed her worries. Lots of people came through this station. It was probably just a coincidence.

She kept a good distance between her and the woman, not so sure anymore that she wanted to talk to her. Her stomach became heavier and heavier the closer they got to Michal's home. Michal stopped a few doors down and watched her double. She took out a set of keys identical to hers from the tote bag she'd bought last spring and unlocked the door. Michal stood rooted to the pavement, her brain half-processing the other woman calling out from the entrance in English to Michal's kids, her voice reminding Michal of watching videos of herself. A dark tide began to rise inside her body as she watched the door of her home shut, leaving her outside.

She just stood there, her brain refusing to talk to her muscles.

After a while, she managed to cross the street to get a view into the house. She peered through the window for what felt like hours, watching the living room of her own house like a film. Their windows were the only ones on the block open. She knew people could look in, but she couldn't bear the feeling of a closed-off house. Each morning, like back home, she would throw open all the shutters and windows to let the fresh air in.

Now, she looked inside and watched herself moving around the house, reclining on the arm of the sofa by the window and reading at her favourite reading spot. Out of old habits, she reprimanded herself for not finishing up the laundry before sitting down to read. The disapproving voice in her head was her grandmother's. Michal wondered whether the doppelganger could hear her granny's admonitions, too.

Dark clouds gathered. A torrential autumn rain began pelting her. She pulled out the umbrella she was used to carrying now, even on sunny days. People walked past her, their shoulders up to their ears, their heads bowed against the rain. The gutters turned swiftly into a river, the water streaming down the street. She could imagine the spreading muddy pool that would be created at the intersection, the water's charge coming to a halt at the ineffectual sewer. The setting sun painted the heavy drops gold and red.

Michal watched the doppelganger go into the kitchen as darkness crowded her. She saw Layla and Eli coming down from their bedrooms after showers to watch TV. Her dark eyes followed them as they got up from the sofas and went into the dining room for supper, hugging the stranger on the way. Her diaphragm felt tight, and every muscle in her body screamed at her children to be careful. They didn't recognise the woman as an impostor. They looked happier than they had in months.

There were no arguments, Michal noticed. She started to doubt herself. Perhaps this wasn't her house? Perhaps *she* was the impostor who had followed this nice lady home. When the streetlights woke up with a start, she realised she didn't know where she would sleep that night.

Still unable to determine how to confront the situation, Michal decided she'd find a room for the night. Maybe she'd wake in the morning and find this was all a dream. Maybe the last five years had all been a dream, including the ridiculous pandemic. Reality hadn't been real in a while now.

Maybe when she woke, Michael would find that she was still in Israel, sharing a bed with her mother to stay close to her grandmother's *shivaa*. She'd put the kettle on, pour boiling water over the weak instant coffee, sip and grimace. Then she'd go back to her grandmother's house where she'd spend the day being nice to old people she hadn't seen since her childhood and making sure her mother had had something to eat.

She stood a little while longer, unable to tear herself away from the doppelganger and her kids as they cracked open a board game in the living room. The other woman seemed to have endless patience for them.

Michal only realised she was waiting for James to come home when he unlocked the door and walked in. She watched the golden window as he walked into the living room, hugged Layla, ruffled Eli's hair and kissed the other woman hello. She watched him gaze into her eyes, recognising the look. Then the impostor and James disappeared into the kitchen, where she no doubt was heating a plate for him and listening to his day.

Michal felt the sullen tide of disappointment filling every crevice of her body. She took a deep breath and fished her phone out, locating a decent hotel close by. Her brain wasn't working properly, she knew that much. She needed to keep her head above the water. A good night's sleep would make everything better. She prayed her credit cards still worked.

She woke in a strange hotel room with the feeling that her skin was half a size too small. She dressed in yesterday's clothes and ran the tap. Then she pooled the water in her hands, closed her eyes and washed the nightmares away, feeling the cool water flowing down her face, childhood memories reverberating through her bones. The time she confessed her love to her fellow classmate and was rejected in the stabbing cruelty reserved for eight-year-old boys. The time a strange older man tried to convince her to come with him at the regional bus station instead of taking the bus to her grandmother's house. Her grandfather picking her up from kindergarten, the two of them strolling through the little park. She wondered why these memories were suddenly coming to her. Maybe these are the cornerstones of who she is, and her brain was just reviewing the evidence.

She was right, though. The night's sleep and a long espresso from the corner café had snapped her back to who she was. Seeing her familiar face in the mirror on the mouldy hotel bathroom wall had helped, as did the memories.

Michal would go back, reclaim what was hers.

But first, she needed to assess her rival. She needed to understand what the other woman wanted and what would be the best way to get rid of her. She'd go in and catch her when she was alone. Start a conversation. Maybe she didn't even realise she was a doppelganger? Maybe she thought *she* was the original.

Michal waited for James to leave for work and the kids for school. Then she took her keys out and entered as quietly as she could. She went straight into the kitchen. The impostor was cooking. The frying onions whispered on the pan, the smell of garlic tickling her nostrils.

Michal nodded appreciatively. "Hello," she said.

The doppelganger turned around, startled. She stared at Michal with wide eyes. This was the first time they had made eye contact.

Michal felt something like electricity running through her body. She recoiled at the same time as her double. They both sent right hands to the base of their throats simultaneously. It was almost like looking in the mirror, except the other woman was wearing Michal's jeans and one of her weekend tops, which Michal resented, seeing as it was Wednesday.

"What are you doing here?" The doppelgänger asked.

"What, you thought I'd just give up?"

The doppelganger pursed her lips.

"Who are you? Where did you come from?" Michal was never one to beat around the bush.

"I'm you, obviously. Anything else doesn't matter."

"But *I'm* me." Michal hates the way her own voice sounds. Like she's pleading.

"So, you say."

"What do you mean 'so you say'? Who says you're me?"

"Family seems happy enough."

Michal felt her confidence wobble. That woman had played a board game with the kids rather than just letting them watch TV all evening. She tightened her tummy and edged her heels outward, grounding herself like in yoga class.

"A board game doesn't make you a good mum."

"They liked my cooking, too. Said it was the best dinner ever. Even James."

"He always says that. He's trying to rally the kids up."

"He didn't even need hot sauce."

Michal gasped for air, drowning. "What do you want?"

"I have what I want," the woman's chin rose, "the question is what do *you* want?"

"I want my life back, obviously. You can't just walk into my house and take over."

"Who says it's your house? Who says it's your life?"

Michal crossed her arms over her diaphragm, her eyes narrowed. The doppelganger lifted her eyebrows.

"I was here first."

She gave the age-old answer of colonisers. "I'm here *now*."

Michal's defiant crossed arms turned into a pitiful self-hug.

"They'll find you out eventually."

"Maybe. Maybe not. Maybe by the time they notice, they'll just think I've changed a little."

Michal looked around the unusually tidy kitchen, the minimalist living room behind the opening. She noticed the impostor had kept a glass of water on the kitchen table, like she did. She couldn't bear to be here a second longer, with this woman who was a complete stranger, but also not.

Michal walked silently to the front door. She kept her keys. Maybe later she'd feel stronger, less adrift. She spent the rest of the day standing outside, like the day before. But instead of being blank, her mind was racing.

She came up with six hundred and thirty-eight plans of action and had dismissed them all by the time James came home from work that evening. How do you prove you are you? How do you even know who you are anyway? She thought about her conversation with Eva, when Eva fired her. She had said Michal "had a tendency towards confrontations". But Michal didn't feel confrontational; she felt opinionated. Who was right? She thought about the times she'd hug Brits who weren't ready for such closeness. They saw her as a warm person, but it was just how she grew up. Was she a warm person or had she failed to integrate, like oil on water?

She saw James walking from the tube station side of the street towards the house. She was standing a few doors down and on the other side, and he never looked up. As she watched him unlock the door and enter the house, her plan clicked into place in her brain. Beyond being her partner, James was her best friend. He knew her better than she knew herself. He would recognise her. He must.

She knocked on the cobalt door. James opened it. She could feel the darkness at her back, a physical presence ushering her in, but she couldn't cross the threshold. He stared at her, silent, eyes wide, for a long time. Then looked to the kitchen, trying to catch a glimpse of the doppelgänger.

"You look awfully like my wife," he said when he looked back.

"I am your wife, you idiot."

"You say that, but I've come from the kitchen, where my wife is sitting right now. So, unless this is some crazy sci-fi alternate universe shit, which last time I checked it wasn't, you are definitely, one hundred percent *not* my wife."

"You're not even gonna invite me in?"

"Lady, I don't even know what's going on. Why would I let you into my house?"

"How can you say that? We've been married fourteen years." Michal's confidence was draining dangerously. Soon, she, too, would drain and disappear, leaving a dried husk.

"I've been married to my *wife* for fourteen years."

"Can you at least call her? Please?"

"Hold on." He said, then called for her, looking back into the house.

The doppelganger appeared in the hallway. Michal felt the jolt of electricity again but was ready for it this time. The other woman stared at her, then a hint of a smirk flashed in her eyes.

"Why are you talking to the crazy lady?" she asked James.

"You know this lady?"

"Yeah, don't you remember I told you I met a crazy lady who looked exactly like me?"

"No, when did you tell me that?"

"Oh, ages ago, before I was fired. I met her in the city. You don't remember? I guess she still lives around there and followed me home yesterday when I went to the job interview."

"The job interview was at your old office?"

"No, you twat, a couple of blocks away. Must have seen me on the street. Remember I told you about her? She was saying she's me?"

"But ..." James looked from Michal to her double.

"Look, lady," the woman took over, "if you don't leave, we'll call the police. This is not your home. Go away."

"Wait," he said, his eyes kind, "what's your name?" James was a sucker for life's wretched. He was forever bringing home maimed hedgehogs and fallen chicks, patching them up, setting them free. For once, this might play to her advantage. As Michal's heartbeat quickened, she almost thought all those animal rescues were worth it.

"My name is Michal," she answered, her lips chapped. Then, a flash of an idea. "Why don't you ask her what her name is?" she jerked her chin towards the doppelganger. James looked back.

"Seriously?" The doppelgänger's eyebrows shot up her forehead. I need to use more lotion, Michal thought.

"It's a fair question, given the situation." His voice was remarkably steady.

The woman stood silent for a long time; her arms crossed. Then she nodded to Michal, which Michal thought meant something like "well played". Then she stepped past Michal and disappeared into the night.

James looked at Michal, his black eyes wide.

"Come on," she said, entering her home, caressing his cheek on the way, "let's not stand in the doorway like idiots."

She hung her tote bag on the entrance hook. "Ugh, that bitch took my favourite top."

AUTHOR BIOGRAPHY

Gal Podjarny is a student of the human psyche and condition. With a background in psychology and academic writing, her fiction explores the intricacies of identity and the roles we assume in the tapestry of relationships. Her first short stories collection, *Human Fragments*, is now out in digital stores, and you can catch her musings on her blog at www.galpod.com.

Round peg in a square hole

by Padmini Sankar

◆◆◆◆

Pramila's reflection stared back at her from the ornate mirror beside the front door. She examined herself with one eye half-closed. Hair in place, check; lipstick not bleeding, check; cheeks highlighted, check. The high-street skirt was a tad too tight, her legs too spindly, but she'd pass. That exercise regimen couldn't alter genes.

"I'm going," she yelled, and without waiting for a reply slipped out of the door, letting it bang shut. Mohan could get his own breakfast. He didn't have a pressure-cooker of a job like hers, selling and renting real estate.

She entered the office, to the usual chatter and laughs. Mandy was holding sway, the girls clustered around her. There were peals of laughter.

Pramila switched on the kettle to make herself a cup of tea. What a faux-pas she'd made that first time – was it just a year ago? Filling the kettle with tap water. One of the girls had screamed, "Eek! We'll all die of germs if you use that water." She never forgot that 'eek.'

She'd obediently emptied the kettle and filled it with the 'good' water from the dispenser. She wanted to argue, say it was boiled and any bacteria would die, sizzled to nothingness at 100 degrees Fahrenheit. But she held back her words. No, she wanted to be part of this group so badly. This job was so precious for her, not just because of the big commissions, but also because it was a multinational real estate company with branches in many countries. Her colleagues, an all-female team, looked as if they'd stepped out of the pages of Vogue or Vanity Fair. Although the youngest was thirty-five and the oldest fifty-five, they were collectively called "the girls."

Pramila had undergone a metamorphosis of sorts after joining the company. Her hair was regularly cut by a Lebanese man in a saloon with a French-sounding name she could never quite pronounce. She exercised daily, running, weights, the works, and swam ten laps every weekend at the club pool of which she'd become a member. It all cost money, of course, but she'd convinced her husband to take out a loan. "It'll pay off, I'm telling you, "She'd said.

She was no longer Pramila Parmanand but Pramila Anand or just Prams. Short, crisp, easy to say.

But Paradise was quite different from what she'd expected. She realized very soon that she could never be part of this group no matter how hard she tried. Was it a cultural divide? East is East and West is West and all that blah? Probably. But a prickly ball of red anger rose in her when she felt completely and utterly invisible. When they laughed and chatted as if she did not exist. Made plans for lunch, gave each other little presents on birthdays, exchanged notes on the best hairstylist in town, and so on. The Invisible Woman. That's how she referred to herself.

"The coven of witches!" she thought angrily. Or should she call them bitches? They had now stopped all pretence of even including her. Even when she entered the office, when they were all chatting and laughing, no one said a hi to her. Or only sometimes. Like she was a stray dog to whom you throw a half-eaten sandwich or a dry chapatti.

It was Mandy who was behind it all. Amanda Nelson was her real name. The whole day she got used to the girls saying Mandy this and Mandy that. Mandy was their leader, both officially and unofficially, and they doted on her. She drove a Porsche convertible and didn't really need this job, but she was a good seller. All the exclusive clients came to her. The ones with fat expat packages, their faces still red from the Dubai heat which they were just getting used to. It was Mandy who'd smoothen their settling in, not just with finding the ideal villa with pink bougainvillea pouring over whitewashed walls, but also the thousand and one other things they needed to know to make their stay just like "home." Where to get the best pork sausages or sundowners, what schools to put their children in, where to get rhubarb pie or jam roly-poly, what was a good substitute for Bisto gravy granules. (Oh, so hard to get! Disappears as soon as it finds its way to the supermarket shelves.) Yes, Mandy had all the answers to questions known and unknown, and was a favourite of the boss too. Mr. Harold Jenkins, a tall man with a beer belly, openly flirted with her and with all the girls. Except of course Pramila, who he treated with polite respect. Why oh why didn't he flirt with her? She could easily come up with clever, witty rejoinders, just like the others.

It was Mandy who sent out the girls on their various assignments, doling out different areas to them so there were no fights. To Pramila she always gave the Karama and Deira areas where the rents were never as high as the Palm or the Ranches. She was always left dealing with the Asian clientele, the ones who came like her for the Dubai dream, mid-level managers or small business owners, men with potbellies and ugly leers who she'd quickly put in place. She was not *that* kind of girl! The tight set of her mouth, her aloof body language, would tell them to eff off in no uncertain terms. She was sick to death of dealing with them.

"Why can't I change areas? I can do the Springs instead," she told Mandy.

"My dear," Mandy sat her down, looking at her sternly and kindly over her Prada reading glasses. "no one else but you can do this job. This is the hardest area to rent out. No, none of these other girls have the push that you have. They'll make a disaster of it!"

Mandy knew this was a lie. The "good" areas were hands-off for her. Why? Because of the colour of her skin? Because she didn't speak with the right accent?

But Pramila was making enough on the rentals -- maybe not as much as the other girls, but still a sizeable amount – so she clamped her mouth shut. She kept reminding herself that she was here for the money and couldn't care less about her colleagues. That's what she told her sister Gayatri who she called up every week. Gayatri, older to her by three years, was her guide and mentor. An Ayurvedic doctor by profession, Gayatri had rejected marriage in favour of service to society. Calm, dependable Gayatri -- such an antithesis to Pramila!

"Well, why do you sound so angry then?" she asked Pramila.

Pramila thought for a moment. Yes, she couldn't well ignore this treatment. The last week had been the worst by far. The girls had planned a beach party, and the discussions took place loud and clear in her hearing.

"So, Jumeirah beach this Saturday?"

"Ooh, get your bikinis out!"

"There aren't any peeping Toms are there?"

"Huh! Dubai without its share of creeps! Of course, there must be. But it's ok. I was there last week."

"Kevin'll really enjoy lazing in the sun."

"Yeah, and Bob can join him. With a few Heinekins."

They had walked out together, discussing the party, and hadn't even bothered to say bye to her as she sat at her desk. It was as if she didn't exist.

She told Gayatri the whole story. "Gaya, I'm just sick of them."

Gayatri listened to her younger sister patiently.

"Look, just ignore them. They don't know any better. Would you even go with them if you were invited?"

Of course, she wouldn't. Pramila knew that.

But her sister's saintly advice fell on deaf ears. Her anger stewed within her. And it was mainly directed at Mandy. It was Mandy who instigated the group, and only Mandy could set things right. But Mandy was the worst of the lot, snubbing Pramila outright, not listening to her suggestions, not even acknowledging her existence. Bright, cheerful Mandy who all the girls loved. They hero-worshipped her, they did! Pramila couldn't sleep well these nights. She was seething with anger. And the worse thing was she couldn't even tell her boss, it was pointless approaching him with her complaint. What argument did she have? That the girls were leaving her out of their conversations, going out for lunch together, meeting after office hours, attending concerts and shows? He'd think she'd gone off her rocker. Worse still, he'd think she was culturally a bad mixer. No, she couldn't go to him.

But something had to be done if she were to retain her sanity. She'd teach that bitch Amanda a lesson!

The next day, after work, she sent her husband out to the supermarket with a long list, claiming she was too tired to accompany him. When he'd left, she made a call.

"Gaya, are you free to talk?" She could hear over the line the whirr of the old fan that sent out hot blasts of air, and heard some murmured conversation in the background.

"Parmu, is that you? Just hold on for a minute." Gayatri's voice was just as it always was – soft, balanced, not too loud. Just like Gayatri herself.

How could two sisters be so different, Pramila sometimes wondered. Gaya was good-natured, a good listener, and as balanced as all the doshas she set right in her patients. Appa had been so proud of her.

But Pramila? She had been the younger, more frivolous one. People said it came with the territory, being the younger one. It was as if she had a right to throw tantrums and get her way, especially as their mother had died shortly after she was born. She was pitied, much more than Gaya. Poor girl. She wouldn't even remember her mother, although the elder child would carry some memories.

Pramila liked all the good things of life, the little luxuries that were always beyond their middle-class reach. Not like Gaya. Always in a khadi kurta or a handloom sari, she had pursued her ambitions single-mindedly.

Not that Pramila was jealous of Gaya. No, quite the contrary. She doted on her elder sister, always seeking out her opinion. Gaya had refused to marry, but Pramila had married, a nice boy working in

Dubai (picked out from shaadi.com, the best matrimonial website) whose mother waved his MBA degree in their faces when he came to 'see' Pramila. Dubai beckoned. Pramila agreed to the match.

Gaya came back on the line. "It's been really busy today, Parmu. Yesterday we were closed for Krishna Jayanti."

Pramila looked at her watch. It was seven-thirty Dubai time, which meant it was nine pm in India. "My goodness, Gaya, you really work late!"

"It's OK," said Gaya. "Appa's had his dinner. I'll have mine soon." Her office was in one of the front rooms of their ancestral house, an old-fashioned bungalow with a tiled roof and a huge kitchen garden at the back where Gaya grew her herbs. "How's the office going?"

"It's fine," Pramila said shortly. She'd decided not to tell her sister what was troubling her. She was in no mood to listen to one of Gaya's goody-goody sermons. She had to take action.

"Gaya, can you suggest a medicine that is tasteless. I keep getting stomach cramps during my period. Remember you gave me one the last time I was there, some powder you mix with water?"

"Oh, you mean xxxxxx kashayam?" Gayatri rattled off an unpronounceable name. "Are you sure you need that? Remember it gives you very bad body odour."

"I'll take it on weekends," said Pramila. "That's the only one that helps. How fast can you ship it to me?"

Gayatri, ever the obliging sister, promised to ship it to her the very next day.

"Send me enough for six months," said Pramila. "Then I don't have to keep asking you."

The package arrived within a week. The very next day, when

the coven had disappeared for lunch, Pramila went into action. All the girls kept a big glass of water on their tables. Amanda had one of those Starbucks' waterglasses, with a cover and a plastic straw wedged through the middle. It didn't take long for Pramila to whip off the cover and throw something in, which she stirred vigorously with the straw, and then recapped. It was a herbal powder, colourless, tasteless, and (thank goodness) easily dissolvable. Pramila waited to see the fun.

Pramila noticed with satisfaction how one of the girls moved a little away shortly after Mandy had downed her glass. It was just a small movement, but she knew the herbal powder was doing its job.

"Ah, wicked wicked me!" she thought joyfully. Just that one small movement told her so much.

It was easy to pop a pinch or two into Mandy's water. She was never at the office for lunch but always out, either taking a client for a viewing or out with the girls. And her glass was always topped with water. It became routine for Pramila. Morning viewings over, she'd return to an empty office for lunch and go through the motion: whip off, add, stir, close, return to desk and eat her lunch alone. She was careful not to add too much and also to sometimes leave a day free in between. She called those days add-free days and laughed at her own little private joke.

As the days went on, everyone in the office began noting Mandy's foul odour. Especially after lunch, but sometimes even in the mornings. And soon the whispering started...

It was not long before Mandy realized that people were moving away from her, even avoiding lunch with her. Her clients never called her back. Pramila noted how thin and worried and, yes, old, she had suddenly become. The wrinkles on her forehead were now more prominent.

Then one of her cronies gently suggested that she see a doctor to rule out any health problems. It was Charlotte, the no-nonsense in charge of the complex legal and financial documentation, who brought it up.

"We all suffer from halitosis sometime or the other, Mandy. You better do something about it!"

Pramila was happy to see Mandy's stricken face. The other girls looked at her sympathetically.

"It'll be fine, Mandy," said one of them, and they all echoed her words. Except for Pramila who pretended to be absorbed in something on her laptop, although her ears were pricked.

"I know a very good doc in Healthcare City. I can take you there. You needn't drive," Charlotte offered.

Mandy broke down. "I-I just don't know what's happening. Steve's been really nice about things but now we don't even share the same bedroom. He just quietly leaves after I've fallen asleep and goes into the sitting room and sleeps on the sofa. And then, early morning he returns. He thinks I don't know but I do." Here, Pramila noticed with satisfaction the tears streaming out of Mandy's eyes.

"Maybe it's your diet," she broke in on their conversation. "I heard you mentioning halitosis." She knew that wasn't a very helpful thing to say, but it felt awkward, during this time of girly camaraderie, for her to keep quiet.

"Her diet hasn't changed," Charlotte said shortly. Then once again, they cut her out of their circle just as if she were a pustule that was excised, and the pep talk continued. Pramila knew the foul smell wasn't just coming from Mandy's mouth but from her entire body. From every single pore.

"She's been admitted into the ICU."

"Oh my god! The poor girl."

"Seems she just collapsed, the poor thing, when she reached home. Started blabbering incoherently. Something about wanting to kill herself."

"Mandy? I can't believe she'd ever say a thing like that! See what sickness can drive you to."

The girls were clustered around the teakettle. They were speaking in low, sombre tones. When Pramila entered, a little late that morning, she immediately knew that something serious had happened.

"Where's Mandy?" she asked.

"Al Zahra hospital. On a drip." Charlotte answered.

Pramila felt a pang of remorse. The previous two days, she'd added a more generous dose of the powder.

"Yes, she wasn't feeling well. I guess you must have noticed too."

"I-is she going to be OK?"

"God only knows," Charlotte said in a voice that spelt doom and gloom. "Steve's in a right royal state. Doesn't know what's happening to her."

Just then Mr. Jenkins entered.

"It's not good news I'm afraid. Mandy's been put on a ventilator. Her organs are shutting down."

Everyone was silent with shock.

"I think you all know what you're supposed to be doing today. So just carry on with your work." With another sad smile, he left the room.

Arabian Noir

Pramila excused herself and said she had to use the restroom. Once there, she first made sure no one was present in any of the cubicles. Then she called up Gaya.

"Parmu, at this time?" Her sister was surprised as Pramila usually called up in the late afternoon or evening. "I've got a patient waiting outside so can you call me later?"

"Gaya, this is urgent." Pramila's voice came out in a breathy tone. "Remember that powder you gave me? The one for stomach pain?"

"Yes."

"Well, what do you do if you've taken too much of it?"

"Parmu, you don't sound as if you've taken too much. You wouldn't be talking to me now if that were the case. Too much of that will give you heart palpitations, maybe even a stroke, I told you not to use it for more than a week."

"Yes, Gaya, it's not me." Gaya waited for her to clarify. "Look, I can't explain right now, but is there an antidote to someone who takes too much?"

"Parmu, don't tell me you've given it to one of your friends," Gaya said. Pramila could sense the disapproval in her voice. "These are controlled Ayurvedic drugs, and really dangerous if taken in excess."

"Please Gaya, just answer my question. I'll explain everything later."

"Nothing really. Just lots of water to flush the kashayam from your system."

Pramila cut the phone shakily.

If something happened to Mandy, she'd be a murderer. Perhaps there'd be a post-mortem, and traces of the herbal remedy would be found in her system? It wouldn't take a police detective very long to

Arabian Noir

put two and two together. Not only would she be caught, but her poor innocent sister would also be implicated.

Pramila's mouth was dry, and her mind a nest of wasps. Oh, why on earth had she decided on this silly mode of revenge? Come to think of it, Mandy had merely done her job in assigning territories to the girls, and she had done it well. Pramila was making enough from the rentals. The ladies were not that bad. It couldn't be helped that they were friends, and she could never fit in.

"Hey, you look pale, love! Are you OK?" Charlotte cut into her thoughts,

"I-I'm fine."

"Here, drink up." Charlotte filled up her glass with cold water from the dispenser and brought it to her workstation. Pramila gulped down the water. It didn't do much in calming her nerves. Her heart continued to beat as if it were in a running match. It was painful. Almost as if it would burst out from her body, spurting red all over the floor.

"I think you better just call it a day and go home. Are there any viewings lined up today?"

"N-no, not really."

"Okeydokes, then run along and I'll take care," said Charlotte kindly.

Pramila thanked her and got up to leave. She had the powder bottle in a drawer of her desk and wondered how she'd take it out. Pretending to tidy things up, she waited for Charlotte's back to be turned and then grabbed the bottle and stuffed it into her handbag.

Pramila spent a sleepless night, tossing and turning in her bed. Maybe now that Mandy was not being given the drug she'd recover? The doctors would just put it down to a nervous breakdown?

She shakily dressed the next morning and took a cab to work. She couldn't risk driving herself in this state. Charlotte was there, crying, along with Victoria, Zahra and Isabella. They were huddled together in a circle, tears streaming down their faces. Her worst nightmare had come true! Her voice came out in a strange high pitch.

"What happened to Mandy?"

"S-she passed away."

"Oh my god! When?"

"This morning. At 3 a.m. It seems Steve was by her side all through the night."

Pramila collapsed into her chair. Her heart seemed to have become five kilos heavier, and she could hear it go thump-thump-thump in her chest. Oh, if only she could have a heart attack right now and collapse and die. Should she just make a clean breast of things and own up? Tell the police what she had done, her part in Mandy's death? They'd find out sooner or later. What would be the punishment? Death? Life imprisonment? Her poor father would certainly die when he learnt the news. Her sister's career would come to an end. Who would go to a doctor who was the sister of a murderer? Her husband, her poor innocent husband, would be unnecessarily implicated. He'd be beaten up, made to confess, a motive ascribed to him. She felt her throat muscles choking.

There was a knock on the door, and Mr. Jenkins walked in with a police officer.

"Ladies, this is Chief Inspector Ayman Abbas. He'd just like to ask you all some routine questions. I want you to see him one by one. He'll be in the next room." Bob's face looked grave. "Please, ladies, I want you to remember and recall very carefully everything that

Mandy said and did this last month or even before. Report anything strange you noticed, even if it's the most unimportant thing."

The girls trooped in one by one. Some of them spent ten minutes, one or two an entire hour in that room. Pramila's turn came last. It was almost two pm when she knocked on the door and was told to enter.

"Mrs. Parmanand, please take a seat." The officer's English was surprisingly clear, and he spoke with a clipped British accent. It was obvious that he had spent many years in the UK.

Ayman Abbas asked her routine questions, all of which were recorded on a small, powerful-looking camcorder.

"Mrs. Parmanand, did you notice anything strange in Mrs. Amanda Nelson's behaviour?"

He had started the interrogation,

"Yes, yes. She seemed to be suffering from bad body odour."

"Did you notice this yourself?"

"N-no, I sit far away from her."

"Then how do you know she had body odour."

Pramila swallowed nervously. Had she said too much, let out stuff she shouldn't have said.

"I-I heard the others talking about it."

"Who did you hear talking about it?"

"Well, Charlotte once told her that she had halitosis, and she knew a very good doctor in Healthcare City, and she'd take her."

"Halitosis? But that is bad breath. You mentioned bad body odour."

Pramila's heart began fluttering. Her mouth felt dry, and she wished she could have a cold sip of water. But the officer with his all-seeing eagle eyes was waiting for her response.

"I-I'm sorry. Maybe she had halitosis. I've confused it with body odour. I'm not sure really, what she had, but she definitely wasn't feeling her usual self."

The officer heard her explanation patiently. She answered a few more routine questions, and the interrogation was over.

The next few days passed in a whirl. She attended office robotically, did her work, took a couple of clients around for a viewing. She even managed to take a client who was interested in a villa in Arabian Ranches. With Mandy gone, everything was haphazard, and Charlotte, who had been reinstated in her place, was still learning the ropes.

Pramila spent a week or two in a roiling nightmare. Work gave her an opportunity to keep her mind off the black thoughts that plagued it. But after work, she became quiet, reclusive, sitting in silence for hours together, not even watching one of the inane serials she used to love watching, crashing into the sofa with one of the springs missing and adjusting her bottom comfortably, remote in hand and a big bowl of Bombay mixture by her side. Apart from work-related calls, she stopped speaking to anyone. Her husband put it down to office stress.

The girls in her office planned to visit Steve to pay their condolences. With Mandy gone, everyone seemed to have changed, and the old girly exclusiveness had vanished.

"We'll all visit Steve tomorrow afternoon at five. Is that OK with you?" Charlotte asked. Pramila was pleasantly surprised. She wasn't asked if she'd like to join. It was assumed that she would join. This was an important distinction to her. She was now one of them.

"Yes of course," she answered. Then wondered if she were doing the right thing. Would she be able to face Steve? After what she had done?

The next day, just two short weeks after Mandy had died, the girls, all discreetly dressed in sober tones, went with a huge bouquet of white lilies to Steve's villa in Barsha.

Steve opened the door to them, still bleary-eyed and unshaven, and ushered them into the tastefully decorated living room. Mandy's hand was written all over it, from the chintzy curtains to the funky sofas and the art-deco pieces that were scattered about the room.

They spoke of all the things Mandy had done for them, said every good thing about her, said things were not the same without her, the usual things people say about the dear departed. Steve heard it all. Then he spoke.

"I don't know if you were aware, but Mandy was taking some kind of herbal supplement." Here, he took a big gulp of water. Pramila froze into her chair, her body trembling slightly. The girls waited for him to go on.

"S-she never told me." Here, two tears slipped out of the corners of his eyes. "But the doctors found out when they did the post-mortem."

Charlotte got up and went to pat Steve reassuringly. He seemed to derive strength from that and continued.

"It was such a huge tumour! And she kept it to herself. The stupid thing was taking some herbal supplement to cure it. And I just thought she had bad body odour and used to move out and sleep every night on the couch. If only I'd known!" Steve covered his face with his hands.

Pramila felt such a rush of relief that she almost shouted out. The heaviness in her head immediately disappeared, and her heart too felt lighter.

"She never told us!" said Charlotte. "And we girls would discuss everything under the sun, including all our real or imagined ailments."

"It was one of those fast-growing tumours," said Steve, "and I don't know whether she really knew what it was. She may have had some stomach cramps. The doc told me that's what it shows up as, and there'd be no other symptoms."

Pramila let out a small involuntary cry.

"Are you all right, lovey?" asked Charlotte.

"I'm fine," said Pramila, her face deathly pale.

◆◆◆◆

Pramila's work continued as before. But she now no longer wore fashionable high street clothes, nor did she complain about the area allocated to her. Somehow, the spring had gone from her step.

AUTHOR BIOGRAPHY

Padmini's debut novel, *The Mother of all Parties* (published by Black Ink, an imprint of HarperCollins), is a fun romp through the life of a Dubai socialite. She's completed the sequel as well as a middle-grade children's fantasy. Padmini's short story was a finalist in the Historical Writers' Association's Dorothy Dunnett Competition and published in their anthology. Padmini lives in Dubai with her husband and enjoys reading, travelling, cooking (she claims to make the best gunpowder masala in town), or else having a good chinwag with her friends. She is presently gathering material for a historical novel set during World War 2. You can find out more at: https://www.padminisankar.com

Solid Evidence

A Detective Inspector Williamson Mystery by Paul A. Freeman

••••

In the conference room cum ballroom of Doha's Rotunda Hotel, Detective Inspector Williamson was fighting a losing battle against boredom, jetlag and the urge to nod off. The air-conditioning was down low, over-compensating for the broiling Arabian sun outside and was another reason he had trouble keeping his eyes open.

Once again, he had been chosen as the 'lucky' police officer to represent the British constabulary at the International Conference of Crime Fighters. This time it was being held in Qatar, a peninsular nation dangling off the Arabian Peninsula. Attendance was a dubious honour, and as before he was being forced to sit through one interminable presentation after another.

A grinning waiter appeared, dressed in baggy pantaloons, a ballooning, vivid red shirt and a turban, and looking like a character from the Arabian Nights. He poured Williamson a tiny, handleless cup of Arabic coffee which smelled and tasted, ironically, of cardamom. However, it woke him up like a double shot of espresso.

The Indonesian delegate came to the end of her talk on the illegal logging of rainforests, and Williamson, now buzzing, roused himself long enough to clap politely.

Arabian Noir

"That will be all for today, ladies and gentlemen," said the master of ceremonies, an exuberant Arab policewoman attired in full ceremonial uniform, her hair tucked modestly beneath a *shayla*. "Tomorrow, at nine o'clock sharp, we shall begin our second day's session with a presentation from our esteemed British colleague, Detective Inspector Jack Williamson. I'm sure we're all looking forward to that."

Another round of polite applause filled the conference room. Williamson gave a nonchalant nod and a wave to identify himself and felt himself blushing. He was unused to speaking in front of an audience; besides which, he did not have a clue yet as to what he was going to talk about. Divine inspiration was on hand however, and as the delegates filed out of the conference room, an Asian gentleman with a briefcase ambushed him.

"Doctor Ashok Baghwali," said the stranger, extending his hand.

Williamson regarded the man suspiciously for a second. He was middle aged, had an intense stare, and had an annoying habit of twitching his grey moustache from side to side like a hairy pendulum.

"Can I help you, doctor?" said Williamson, shaking the man's hand.

"Murder! It was murder, I tell you." He raised his briefcase. "I have all the documentation to help you prove it."

"I don't get your drift, sir."

Doctor Baghwali snaked his arm through the crook of Williamson's elbow and guided him to the hotel lobby where Qatari families, dressed in their traditional of white *thobes* for men, and black *abayas* for women, were lounging around enjoying refreshments. He sat the policeman down on a pink sofa garishly embroidered in gold.

"Last year I read a newspaper article about your cleverness in solving the Matherson murder in Southport, England," said Doctor Baghwali. "Who would have known that chewing gum is affected by temperature change, like a body undergoing rigor mortis, thereby allowing an investigator of acuity to determine the time of death? So, when I saw your name on the delegates' list for the International Conference of Crime Fighters, I felt certain you were the one who could assist us."

"Us?"

"The Indian community. Let me explain. Many of my countrymen come to Qatar to better their situation in life. Mostly they sweep the streets or work in construction, carrying bricks and such like. Even so, the opportunities in the Arabian Gulf are better than those back home. Unfortunately, though, due to naivety and ignorance, my countrymen sometimes fall prey to unscrupulous employers who confiscate their passports, exploit them – or worse. And when the worst *does* happen, and one of our compatriots dies, the police investigation of a humble Asian's death is often less than thorough. That's where *we* come into the picture." He reached into his briefcase. "This is the preliminary autopsy report of an unidentified Indian male."

"How do you know he was Indian?" asked Williamson, his interest piquing.

"The man had only rupees in his wallet, and his clothes had labels with 'Made in India' sewn into them."

"Which tells us he must have only just arrived in the country."

Doctor Baghwali's moustache twitched excitedly. "Exactly! You are indeed living up to your reputation."

The detective inspector reluctantly took the proffered autopsy report and leafed through it. His eyes widened as he read. The deceased, an Asian-looking male in his mid-twenties, had apparently frozen to death. He arrived at the morgue completely stiff and took two days to thaw out. The forensic pathologist reckoned the man had also been viciously bludgeoned, though this seemed to have occurred postmortem. Impact marks and fractures indicated a flat, blunt object was used, with much force.

"Virtually every bone in the man's body was broken," said the doctor. "And to be quite frank, the powers-that-be have made a poor show of investigating the case over the past forty-eight hours. They haven't found a single clue, let alone identified a suspect. Nor have they discovered the poor victim's name. In addition, the deceased's fingerprints are not in the nationwide database, even though all new labourers are fingerprinted on arrival at their port of entry. That's why we of the Indian community would like *you* to unravel this little mystery of ours. We want to see that justice is done and whoever perpetrated this diabolical crime is brought to book."

"Did the police check all the meat packaging companies in and around Doha?" Williamson asked. "Perhaps our friend was simply an employee, here illegally, who got locked in a cold room."

"We thought of that, too. But it wouldn't explain the broken bones; not unless he somehow beat himself senseless while trying to keep warm. But with the amount of damage done to his body, that seems very unlikely."

"Indeed!" Williamson flipped over the page of the autopsy report and raised an eyebrow. "It says his body was found in the desert by one 'Doctor Ashok Baghwali'. That makes things easier. Would you mind describing the circumstances under which you discovered the corpse, sir?"

The Indian sat back in the sofa, closed his eyes and after a vigorous twitch of his moustache narrated his strange tale.

"Every Saturday, I, my dear lady wife and my two teenage daughters go camping in the desert, to relax, to get some fresh air and to enjoy the ambience of the desert. We pitch our tents at the base of a sand dune, in the shade of a palm tree, light a fire, barbecue some chicken and sing traditional Indian folk songs."

"Idyllic," said Williamson, hoping to get the man back on track.

"Well, two nights ago I was the last to turn in. I had just doused the campfire when I heard a loud thump from somewhere near the top of the sand dune. Glancing up, I saw an object barrelling towards me. Seconds later I was bowled off my feet by the unidentified dead body in the autopsy report you're holding."

Trying not to snigger at the image of Dr Baghwali being bowled off his feet, Williamson asked, "Did you see anyone else out there in the desert?"

"No. Nor did I hear anything such as a car engine, nor people talking."

Williamson frowned. "Okay, you've hooked me with this little puzzle of yours. We've got until nine o'clock tomorrow morning to solve it, so let's start with you taking me out to the sand dune where this singular event occurred?"

Half an hour before sunset, sitting in the front passenger seat of Doctor Baghwali's all-terrain Land Rover, Williamson arrived at the spot in the Qatari desert where the frozen corpse had come to rest.

Arabian Noir

There were no tangible clues to be discerned at the base of the dune where the doctor had camped, though where the body had rolled down the dune, a trail of impressions still remained visible in the sand.

Next, continuing their investigation of the scene, the two men ascended the steep, leeward slope of the sand dune. Suddenly, the all-embracing silence of the desert was obliterated by the roar of a plane engine.

"We're directly under the flight path to Doha International Airport," the doctor shouted over the racket.

Williamson let out a snort of incredulous laughter. "What a fabulous place to go camping."

Doctor Baghwali ignored the policeman's sarcasm. "The noise keeps other potential campers away. That way we have the place to ourselves. Such solitude far outweighs the occasional disturbance of a passing passenger plane."

At the top of the dune, panting and sweating profusely from the waves of radiant heat, the policeman made a reconnoitre of the immediate area. He then returned to the collapsed section of sand along the dune's sharply defined crest, where the body had rolled down from. There were no footprints in the vicinity from people carrying or dragging the victim. Nor were there any tyre tracks anywhere close by, except those of the Doctor's Land Rover.

"Didn't the police climb up here and have a shufti?" Williamson asked, as the reddening sun disappeared below the desert horizon.

Doctor Baghwali shook his head and pointed to the precipitous ascent the two men had both just scaled. "Our local constabulary and our CID inspectors aren't the most athletic of chaps."

Williamson took out his phone and photographed what he

considered was either a crime scene or a dumping site, or both, and felt at a loss due to the lack of tyre tracks and footprints. "Curiouser and curiouser!" he murmured, and watched thoughtfully as another aircraft made its final, overhead approach to Doha Airport before coming into land. Then a wry smile touched his lips. "If you could take me back to the Rotunda Hotel, I think a couple of phone calls should suffice to solve this case."

At the Rotunda Hotel reception desk, Williamson dialled the number of the local Air India office. Next, acting on the airline's information, the detective inspector put a call though to India, to Mumbai Central Police Station. Minutes later the hotel fax machine was spitting out photographs of Mumbai's most recently reported missing persons.

At the third faxed photograph, Doctor Baghwali's moustache stopped in mid-twitch and his mouth dropped open. "That's him! That's him!" he said and read the name below the picture. "Vinod Sanjit!"

The delegates in the Rotunda Hotel conference room were on the edge of their seats as DI Williamson, from behind the on-stage lectern, recounted the final chapter of his previous evening's exploits.

"The area of sand that had been disturbed along the ridge of the dune told us this was the point from which Vinod Sanjit's frozen and shattered body began its journey down the leeward slope of the dune towards Doctor Baghwali's campsite. However, due to an absence of footprints and tyre tracks, some questions remained. How had Vinod come to be at the top of that sand dune, and why did it look like he had seemingly appeared out of thin air? Then it struck me.

He *had* appeared out of thin air. You see, while I was contemplating the conundrum, a second aircraft flew overhead, its landing gear down as it came into land at Doha Airport. On seeing this, a bizarre notion came to me. Two phone calls later, and my suspicions were confirmed."

The audience in the conference room leaned eagerly forward.

"Firstly, Air India's Doha office informed me that a flight from Mumbai had been making its final approach at about the time Vinod's body crashed into Doctor Baghwali's campsite. Secondly, I called the Mumbai police and asked them to send me pictures of persons recently reported missing. On the third fax we struck lucky."

The Zambian delegate put up his hand. "I still don't understand how Vinod Sanjit got from Mumbai, India, to a sand dune in Qatar."

Williamson shrugged, sadly. "As Doctor Baghwali told me last night, many Indians come to Qatar in search of greener pastures. We can only assume that Vinod wanted to better his financial condition but didn't have a work visa to legally enter the country. He therefore smuggled himself onto an Air India flight to Doha, hiding in the landing gear's wheel housing. However, at thirty thousand feet, where temperatures reach forty below zero, he froze to death. Then, when the landing gear came down as the plane approached the airport, Vinod's body fell to earth, the impact causing multiple bone fractures and spoiling Dr Baghwali's camping trip. No foul play, simply a young man's misadventure."

There was a moment's silence before the conference room erupted in loud applause.

"That's truly amazing, detective inspector!" admitted the master of ceremonies.

Williamson smiled self-consciously as he looked down at one of the mortuary photographs of Vinod Sanjit's frozen corpse. "The evidence was pretty solid."

AUTHOR BIOGRAPHY

Paul Freeman is an English teacher. He authored *Rumours of Ophir*, a crime novel taught at 'O' level in Zimbabwe. He's had two novels, a children's book and an 18,000-word narrative poem published, as well as scores of short stories, poems, and articles. He currently lives and works in Mauritania, Africa.

Miss Pleasance Goes East

by Daisy Line

◆◆◆◆

The view from Patricia's window seat could not be more in contrast with the scene she had left a mere four days ago; the aerodrome at Croydon had been replaced with vast expanses of sandy emptiness. Without the small, shadowed windows, one would be hard pressed to pick out any buildings at all. Settling into her seat, Patricia Pleasance braced herself for another landing.

Since Monday midday she had endured ten successful landings and was just about, she hoped, to survive her eleventh. By aircraft, train, and seaplane she had witnessed, among swirling morning mists, tempting glimpses of olive groves outside Brindisi, watched the dying sun cast shadows through magnificent Acropolis columns and marveled over moonlit pyramids in Cairo; it was a whistle-stop tour of wonders she had hitherto only seen in books. She was entranced.

Patricia, a confident woman, was not averse to risk taking; she had a strident belief in her own abilities. It was the latter facet of her character that led to her being aboard the flight from London to Sharjah that October 1934.

Tolerating the discomfiture was a challenge and one she stoically endured without complaint. She had tried to strike up companionable conversation with the passengers with little success. She expected some reticence from those boarding in Croydon. Being British they were duty bound to keep their air of the aloof Empire elite, but even the loquacious Greek women had snubbed her; by the time they landed in Palestine she was beginning to second guess the prudence of her trip.

In her work-a-day life Miss Pleasence toiled away, albeit in a minor role, at Norland College in Bath. She was responsible for the housing and general duties for the would-be nannies in the making. She never involved herself in the teaching, had no interest in the skills they gained and would not have been a nanny under any circumstances. Therefore, it was a surprise when she was tasked with the collection and delivery of Penelope Caruthers, niece of the world-renowned archeologist Sir Arthur Caruthers, at present on an expedition in the Middle East.

'I've no doubt,' started Miss Winterbotham, the Principal, 'you will carry out this duty with the same care and exactitude you employ as...' here the woman referred to notes, 'our Accommodations Assistant. I have every faith in you.'

Faith she may have, mused Patricia, but matching the obligation to the obligatee, she had little confidence the principal knew what she was about.

Nevertheless Patricia had accepted the responsibility and could not deny the endeavour would afford a welcome break from the drudgery of fulfilling nanny's wants and needs. For reputation's sake a Norland uniform had been hastily purchased from Freeman's as none in the college wardrobe were ample enough for the robust Miss Pleasance. In a small leather folder, a typed itinerary, brown envelopes containing various currencies and a photograph was waiting for her after the trousseaux trip to Kensington. The photograph showed a severe bobbed haircut framing a plump face with the large round eyes of indeterminate colour. The girl looked younger than her 13 years; the school uniform and blank stare did nothing to help. Penciled on the reverse, one word, Penny. Patricia felt sorry for the girl. After the long journey that sympathy had somewhat waned.

As the aircraft filled, being halfway across the world with no tangible support, was starting to put a dint in Patricia's customary self-assurance.

Casting about the cabin, Patricia, although not of the same class as the rest of the passengers, felt she held up pretty well. She had not the easy grace imbued by the brace of husbands and wives that had boarded in Paris and Italy, neither did her womanly attributes match the Grecian beauty of the woman and her daughter from Athens. If just one of them had offered conversation, they would find out she was a worthy companion, less monied, but of excellent breeding.

The couple with her from Croydon looked more uncomfortable the further east they flew; a Mr Robert Hall, and his wife, or so Patricia had assumed at first appraisal. The "wife", a waspish woman given to speaking in low conspiratorial whispers quite irritated Patricia as they were the only other travellers that spoke English.

The remaining passenger held still less hope of companionship. A local gentleman, robed and calm to the point of somnolence, gave a courtly bow on entering the cabin at Basra then proffering no further communication. Already on her third novel Patricia reflected maybe solicitude was not a bad thing per se; one may be apt to talk a mite too much and she had been schooled quite thoroughly on the circumspect nature of her mission.

Answering Patricia's hasty prayers, the landing was uneventful. In the fast-setting sun, they crossed the runway, passing a gathered group of men ready to service the aircraft. Greeted by a stout man, Patricia recognised the Royal Air Force uniform; three stripes on his epilates denoted the rank of sergeant. His florid complexion, waxed moustaches, already drooping in the dusk heat, and jaunty stride stated he was well accustomed to the desert ambience.

'Party all present and correct?' He held a clipboard checking names. 'If you could follow me.' Setting off at a smart pace they headed towards the fort-like structure. Guarded on one side by the air traffic control tower, the rest hid behind high sandstone walls.

Once inside Patricia took in the courtyard enclosed by palm-leaf porticos shading periwinkle blue doors. Occupying the centre, and adding the only other colour to the place, was a small garden oasis giving off the heady scent of jasmine.

The party's progress elicited little notice from several men sitting under the shade of the veranda, concerned as they were in commerce. Patricia noted the scales set on blocks were under particular scrutiny. Whatever they were weighing caused much spirited debate.

'Pearls.' Stated the sergeant as if tapping into Patricia's curiosity. 'Not so much trade these days, the Japanese put paid to that.' Feigning interest, she felt it a curtesy to enquire why. 'Freshwater pearls are all the thing now I'm told; they ship them out by the ton. Torn the arse out of the bona fide market.' He looked abashed and asked pardon for his colourful prose.

'That must have been a blow.' The Halls had stopped to listen. 'I suppose what's left is pretty valuable?'

'Wouldn't know.' The sergeant had opened the first of several doors on the shaded side of the courtyard. 'This is you, Miss Pleasance.' He ushered a small boy through a door bearing her name. Patricia reached into her purse as he struggled with her suitcase.

'Tip is included in your ticket price; I wouldn't give him more.' The sergeant adjusted his moustaches.

'Why?' The boy, overwhelmed with luggage, grinned over the top of her portmanteau.

'He'll make a nuisance of himself.' With that the sergeant left to attend to his other guests. As he made a deep bow in prelude to his leaving, the boy's face rearranged itself into a deep frown.

'Miss Pleasance,' Patricia encouraged.

'Thank you for Mrs Presents.' He palmed the small coins offered, tapped his chest, 'Ahmed.'

Once alone she scanned the small room that was to be her home for the next four days, her confidence made a slight recovery. Comprising whitewashed walls, shuttered window, a cooling breeze from the ceiling fan and an adequate single bed, she needed little else. Although unable to leave the compound, she still had half a dozen books left to read and had packed a small sketch pad; a few days of being waited on, meals provided, and best of all no responsibilities was most welcome.

An early supper, served by Ahmed and several others, was in the Mess. Being introduced to the full complement of Air Force staff was a tad overwhelming. They were a mixture of commissioned and uncommissioned officers, a couple of airmen, the mustachioed sergeant and the Station Commander; bidding her call him, 'James.' She made no reciprocal offer. Her brief was to be wary; first name

Arabian Noir

terms always led to familiarity in her experience.

'Excuses,' another boy hovered by the door. 'Telegram for the madam.' He pointed to Patricia.

'For me? Ladies, gentlemen.' She rose from the table, relieved to be excused from the obligatory small talk, she followed the boy across the courtyard up to the tower.

'Miss Patricia Pleasance?' The airman removed one headphone.

'Yes.'

'Telegram from Sir Caruthers's encampment, marked urgent.'

Reading through the brief message Patricia's heart sank. The girl was arriving early, in a few hours in fact. What she was supposed to do with a prepubescent teenager for four days whilst waiting for the return flight was beyond her. This was not good news.

Brooding, she sat in the courtyard garden trying to sketch the palm trees under lamp light until the heat got the better of her.

'Am I disturbing you?' The rich accent and clipped tones surprised Patricia, for the speaker was none other than the local gentleman absent from supper.

'Not at all, I was about to give up and go back to my room.'

He bowed as before. 'I shall not detain you then. Perhaps we may talk later, let me introduce myself, Abdulla Abbas.'

'Patricia Pleasance, nice to meet you.' For no reason Patricia could identify, she trusted this stranger, so heartily agreed to the meeting.

Retiring to her cabin gave her no rest. The couple next door were in full flow, their flamboyant insults understandable even to those with no knowledge of Italian. Presently a door slammed, voices replaced with dramatic sobs. Against her better judgement Patricia found herself tapping on her neighbour's door. 'Can I come in?'

'Si, do you have drink?'

Patricia apologised for not having such a thing. 'They don't drink here.'

'How bizarre, someone must have something. You could ask.' Feeling coerced, kicking herself for being so stupid as to embroil herself in another's business, she went in search of alcohol.

In the kitchens Patricia found the sergeant who had first greeted them. 'It's not for me, the Italian lady is a bit upset.'

'Yes, Miss Pleasance, we all heard the Amatos. The best I can offer is some homebrew, it's no vintage. Carry it behind your hat.' He handed her a flagon. 'Do you want glasses?'

'One please.' He nodded and she placed the glass in her pocket, shielded the wine with her straw boater and headed back to the room.

It seemed the Amatos had resolved their dispute. As Patricia entered, they were in full embrace. She begged their pardon making for a hasty exit.

'No, please don't go,' pleaded the husband, 'join us, you have been most attentive to my wife.'

Perfect English now I have wine thought Patricia. 'I should give you some privacy.'

'I would be an ungrateful man if I let you run away now, Miss Pleasance is it not?'

'Patricia Pleasance, yes.' From not a sole acknowledging her to this flurry of new connections made her uncomfortable.

'Come, share a drink with us…that is…?'

'Homemade wine I'm told.'

'Perfetto.' Both smiled up at her.

'I'm afraid I only have the one glass.' This, she hoped, could be her excuse. Alas, from a wooden box Signor Amato produced two laboratory beakers and began to fill all three vessels. Lord, though Patricia, I shall have to sip slowly otherwise I shall be in no fit state to meet Penelope.

'What brings you to the desert Miss Pleasance?' asked the Signora.

'A small escort job for my employer,' replied Patricia in an effort to remain vague.

'Escorting who?' It was a direct question from the Signor. *Were Italians always so nosy*? pondered Patricia.

'A young girl related to one of the archeologists out here.'

'Not Sir Arthur by any chance?' Patricia tried to hide her disbelief. 'I see by your face, it is. What a coincidence, we are colleagues and if I may presume, friends of the man.'

The Italian slapped his thigh. 'And this relative, a child I imagine, that is a Norland uniform, yes?'

Not only inquisitive, but well informed; it was time to make her excuses and leave decided Patricia. 'A niece. Now I really must get on, she's arriving soon and I'm unprepared.'

'That is most unusual, I had thought Sir Arthur had, how you say, *niente la sorella*.'

'Perhaps *il fratello*?' responded the Signora.

Patricia was none the wiser as to what they were questioning.

'None, that I know of, perhaps he has an *innamoreto segreto*,' he winked suggestively.

Saving any further confusion, unannounced, the door flung open. 'I was told you were here, Penelope Caruthers, I'm guessing you are Miss Pleasance.'

Somewhat stunned, Patricia shook the proffered hand and with no more ado was dragged from the room as Penelope excused them both with perfect manners.

'All my luggage has been shipped forward, so I've only this.' The girl pointed to a case laid on Patricia's bed. 'Seems like we'll be roommates.'

Casting a doubtful look at the single bed, Patricia could not envisage sharing the cot with this girl, for a start she was a head and shoulders taller than herself.

Penelope laughed. 'Don't fret, we won't be top and tailing,' she held up the valance to reveal the truckle bed beneath. 'We'll be cosy enough. Now, let's get to know one another.'

Patricia, still a mite dazed at the girl's entrance managed a nod. 'I'm Patricia Pleasance, from Norland Collage, I work in administration.'

'Well, I know that. I mean get to know you in the proper sense. Who are your people, where did you grow up?'

Buckling under the girl's exuberance, Patricia answered. 'I grew up in Shropshire, my parents were schoolteachers, I have no brothers or sisters. Is that enough, Penelope?' The girl shot her a look. 'Excuse me, Penny.' The girl recovered her sunny mien and continued with the questions, reaching for a dish of dates placed, Patricia assumed, in her room while she was busy with the Italians.

Mid-question about Patricia's travelling companions, Penny, holding both hands to her chest, began to gasp. Before Patricia could move, her charge slumped to the floor.

'Help, someone help me.'

Through the door burst Abdulla. 'I was afeared something like this would happen. Hold her head.' The girl had started to fit. 'Loosen her collar.'

Obeying with no hesitation, Patricia discovered the girl had bound her chest. This was no teenager. 'I'll have to rip this off.' She looked to her companion.

'No time for ceremony, it's her heart.'

Patricia loosened the binding.

'Now, hands locked, on her sternum, pump...'

Complying, Patricia started compressions. Within a few minutes, the girl had calmed, her limbs ceasing to twitch.

'Is she dead?'

'Can you feel her heartbeat?'

'Yes.' Sweaty, struggling for breath, Patricia seemed in a worse state than the girl laying prone beside her.

'Let's get her onto the bed.' Once settled, Abdulla rose. 'I will not be long. Lock this door and open to no one save me,' he commanded before leaving.

It was all a bit too much; Patricia, overwhelmed, let a tear of frustration escape. 'Come on now,' she chided herself, 'you've more backbone than this.' Wiping her cheek, she went back to attending her patient.

Abdulla, true to his word, returned within a few minutes carrying a pail of water.

The commotion induced several visitors to impose themselves. The Station Commander showed his compassion in a stolid British way, as did the Halls; the Amatos brought the remainder of the wine, the Greeks, Hera and Cora Drakos, arrived staying at the open door, lamented with enthusiasm. Notable by their absence were the Parisians. The last of the callers was Ahmed bringing fresh water and making up the truckle bed.

'She asleep.' He dabbed the girl's head with the gentle touch of a wet cloth.

'She will not wake without assistance.' Abdulla leant forward, lifting one eyelid, the pupil stared out small and fixed.

'She's in a coma,' Patricia said. 'She seemed fit and in rude health when she arrived.' With the room now calm, clarity came to her. 'The dates?'

'I am sure of it, see the rash about her lips. Poison. It is Oleander, all the symptoms fit. I should have been watching, I knew someone would try sabotage. The doctor is away, we are blind, and I am to blame.'

'Now look here Mr Abbas, what *is* going on. I come on this journey to escort Penny to England. First, she turns up 3 days early, then she is no girl at all, now she's poisoned by who knows, fighting for her life on my bed.' Plumping down on the wicker chair, out of steam from the uncommon outburst, Patricia wept. Abdulla let her cry, only handing her a handkerchief to stem the tears.

After a while, when dry whimpers were all, she could manage, he talked. 'You are quite correct; she is no girl. Her name is Araminta Martin, a cohort of mine.'

Patricia did not like the implications "cohort" summoned. 'In what way?'

'We, and I shall have to request this information stay within these walls, are employed by His Majesty to safeguard the Taif Treaty between Saudi and Yemen. The documents Minty was carrying will ensure the continued peace; without them the likelihood is rumours spread by interested parties will go unchallenged and aggravate both countries, peace will fail. I was sent to watch over you both.' He opened Araminta's valise, brought forth a *khanjar* from his waistband and began to cut through the lining.

About to enquire as to which Majesty her companion was referring to, she saw by the royal crest on the papers handed to her it was HRH George V, her own sovereign.

'You have many questions; all I can say is that your good King has been instrumental in finding out who is threatening our accord through the guise of sending Sir Arthur on an expedition and for that I have leant him my allegiance. Miss Martin is my contact, because you can imagine, for me to take these papers to your King would raise many eyebrows as you say. Better we create a more plausible scenario to get the papers to him. With them he can settle the unrest already gathering. We cannot go backwards, we must progress. There is much unrest in the world, things that could upset us all. If we remain fractured, we are weak.'

It was quite a speech. Patricia regarded the woman she now knew as Araminta. 'What are we to do with her?'

'We wait. They will try again to unseat our efforts; we must sit tight. For now, we must keep her comfortable.'

'That might be your solution, not mine.' Patricia had absorbed the information, ordered it in her mind, and her mind told her that to do nothing was no option at all. 'We must find out who it is, who wants these papers and stop them.'

Abdulla smiled. 'You are courageous, like Minty, but that way lays much danger.'

'Danger be damned, I'm not afraid of them. I've a keen mind and you've a sharp dagger. You'd be surprised what skills are required to keep a college full of girls to heel and I'm not about to stand by and let these people win if I can help it.' Her dander was up, her companion impressed.

'What would you have me do?' Abdulla smiled.

'Fetch me Ahmed and his friends.'

Removing their sandals, the boys tiptoed in, their eyes fixed on Miss Martin.

'I want you to tell me who was in the courtyard when I was in with the Signor and Signora, I saw you all going backwards and forwards between the rooms.'

Blinking in response, Abdulla translated for them.

'The Mr Hall was not there, not in room, the woman Hall was on bed in other room.' One boy stuttered.

'So, I was right, they're not married. What about the French couple?' Again,

Abdulla relayed the question.

'With the Sgt Boss, they not happy,' shared Ahmed.

'Go on,' encouraged Abdulla.

'They say plane must go tomorrow. Boss says not possible, engine needs part.'

'I wasn't aware of any problem, but it's convenient none the less. Gives us more time to find the culprits.'

'They want to have car to Sharjah. Boss says no, they have one car, it stays here for supplies and doctor drives. He drives now, babies in Al Mahatta coming. Monsieur is red face cross. Boss's face more red.'

Noting the information in her sketch pad, Patricia added a question mark against the Parisians. 'Which is their room?' Ahmed needed no translation; he pointed across the courtyard. 'You would have seen them if they came anywhere near here.' They all nodded.

'The dates were not in my room when I came back after meeting you Mr Abbas, I'm sure of that. Whoever put them there took advantage of my absence.'

They talked a while longer, ascertaining the Drakos ladies were in the Mess and exonerating most of the lower ranked staff. The call to prayer heralded the departure of the boys and Abdulla for Isha. Patricia, alone behind the locked door, reread her notes. The only people unaccounted for at the time in question were: Mr Hall and Signor Amato for a short while and some of the senior staff. An inside job maybe? There was the mysterious grounding of the aircraft, according to Ahmed a rare occurrence; it may be happenstance or deliberate. She needed to find out. Leaving her room, she blessed the unusual low cloud hiding the moon as she made for the tower.

'Not come for more wine Miss Pleasance? How's your patient?' The sergeant was sipping tea with a couple of his subordinates.

'No and not good I'm afraid.' She enquired as to when their medical man would be returning.

'Who can tell, last time sawbones was out all night and this weather coming in isn't going to encourage him to leave anytime soon. Look,' he handed her binoculars and pointed towards the misty horizon. 'It wouldn't surprise me if we had *shamal* heading our way. Exceptional at night.' He mused to himself.

'We seemed to have brought all manner of bad luck with us. First the plane, then Miss Caruthers, now *shamal*, is that what you called it?'

'Hot winds, yes. You know about the engine then?'

'I do. Anything you can do tonight? I hear the couple from Paris are eager to leave.' She handed back the binoculars.

The sergeant stared at Patricia just a fraction too long for comfort. 'You know rather a lot, Miss Pleasance. I wouldn't have thought it interested you.'

'Circumstances change.'

'You mean you are going forward on the journey?'

'It may be the only chance Penelope has, if I can radio ahead to Gwadar, I may be able to arrange some medical help.'

'I'll do that.' Offered the sergeant. 'Hold on, the things dead. I'll try the telegraph. Nope, nothing. I'll keep trying.'

Another coincidence? Patricia thought not. 'I'll keep you informed of my plans. I must get back to Penny…and thank you for the dates, I've yet to sample them, it was such a generous thought.'

'That was the C.O, thought he'd made a gaff at supper, trying to butter you up.' He called over his shoulder, still tweaking the radio dial.

Patricia could not get down the steps quick enough. An inside job was now definite.

Rounding the courtyard, she heard the front gates open. An ancient truck roared in, skidding feet away from where she stood dazzled by the headlights.

'Where's the patient? I've been on a wild goose chase, there was no birth, then weather had me pinned. Ahmed got a message to me; one of his cousins on a camel, darndest thing.' A slight man, mid-fifties, Gladstone bag in hand peered through his monocle at Patricia.

'Follow me.' The doctor introduced himself and Patricia tried to explain the situation.

'Oleander you say? It's the devil, Desert Rose, we call it.'

'That's what Mr. Abbas suspected. Can you do anything?' Cornering the Station Commander with her accusations would have to wait.

'We need charcoal and warm water, how long has she been like this?' He reached into his bag for his stethoscope.

'About three hours.'

'God's teeth, we may be too late, heartbeat is slow. Go to the stores, charcoal, then the kitchen for warm water; be quick,' he barked. Ahmed and Abdulla returned so Patricia sent the boy for charcoal while she fetched water; both arrived back together.

Unfazed by the doctor's rough tones, Ahmed assisted in breaking the charcoal and mixing it with water. The other two, helpless, watched on; there was little else to do but pray.

'Now I'll need all of you for this, Miss Pleasance, sit her up.' Patricia did as she was bidden, sat behind Araminta, a hand under her chin. 'Mr Abbas hold up the tube, Ahmed pour the liquid and I'll monitor progress.' It was a messy business. By the time they had completed the treatment the room resembled more a tar pit than the tidy space of before.

'Now we wait and hope. I could do with coffee Ahmed, see to it would you.' The boy was gone before the request was complete. 'Would either of you like to get me up to speed on what the bally hell has been going on here?'

Mr. Abbas obliged up to the point when Patricia could hold on no longer. She blurted out a shortened version of her conversation in the tower.

'What do you know of your C.O Doctor Taylor?' asked Abdulla.

'He's alright, a bit of a queer fish, keeps himself to himself but has a genuine connection with the locals.'

'Which locals?' Patricia butted in.

'Not chaps I know, but then I mainly see the women. It's a rum old do, but they seem to trust me.' Mr. Abbas and Patricia exchanged glances.

'It has to be him, but why?'

'There's a sound reason Miss Pleasance.' All three occupants turned. Facing them was Group Captain Pearson, Station Commander and obvious traitor as revealed by the loaded Webley pointing straight at them. 'I was making a fortune supplying both sides with guns, ammunition, that kind of kit, then blow me if they didn't go and make friends. King and country saw fit to place me in this hellhole, why shouldn't I make a few extra bob while I'm stuck here? Now Patricia,' he laboured her name, 'get the papers, bring them here. You'll do nicely for a hostage.'

With a quick glance at Mr. Abbas, she picked up the valise and swung it with all her might. The C.O caught her wrist. 'Now, now, we'll have no heroics. You lot won't be able to leave, I've seen to that. Yes, the engine was my doing, the dates too and as for communicating, the radio and morse telegraph have had a bashing.'

'You rotter, you'll swing for this.' The doctor was incandescent.

Pushing Patricia out towards the truck, his gun still trained on the remaining two, 'You'll have a jolly time soon, old King George will have to send out reinforcements, I'll be sorry to miss the party.'

At that moment, the truck revved, distracting the C.O. The Parisians were making a break for it. Patricia seized the advantage, launching forward to give Abdulla a free run at Pearson. Pinning the traitor to the floor, the point of his *khanjar* at his throat, Patricia relieved the C.O of the gun, leveling it at his head.

'Your coffee Doctor.' Ahmed, arriving seconds late to witness the capture, understood the situation, unwrapped the agal from his head, he secured the prisoner.

Nothing was made of Miss Pleasance when she returned to Bath. In her pocket, she carried a cherished photo of her two new friends and although forbidden to breathe a word of what they had faced together, it gave her comfort. Patricia was, once more, at the beck and call of the Norland nannies.

One fine April morning the following year reception called. 'A lady to see you,' was the message.

'Hello Miss Pleasance,' smiled Araminta Martin, pink cheeked and back to rude health. 'Is there somewhere we can talk?'

'The garden; all the girls are in classes.' Wandering through the tall trees, the noise of the city muted, the air clear as only a spring day can supply, they chatted.

'Of course, they hanged him as a traitor, but it was all hush, hush. Dr Taylor gave evidence as did Mr. Abbas, who sends his best by the way.'

'Did you ever find out why the Parisians were is such a hurry?'

'Yes,' giggled Minty. 'They were on the run, hotly pursued by Madam's husband. Nothing like a cuckolded Frenchman to put fire at your heels.'

'And the Amatos?'

'Illicit pearl smuggling, in league with the Halls. They're still on the run.'

'Were myself and the Drakos ladies the only upright citizens on the plane?'

'Seems so.'

'I've led a sheltered life,' laughed Patricia. 'Are you…?

'Back on duty, yes, but I wanted to come in person to give you this.' She produced a small velvet box. Inside lay a bronze cross bearing the inscription "For Valour."

'Of course, you can't show it to anyone.'

Patricia smiled. 'I wouldn't want to, nothing gained from boasting.'

'If you ever get sick of all this, we could do with someone like you. There's a storm brewing in Europe. It's all hands on deck.'

'I'll think about it.' Patricia pocketed her treasure, bidding Minty goodbye. *I may see you sooner than you think*, she mused, *but for now I must wheedle out the culprit who has been using all Principal Winterbotham's Pears soap.*

AUTHOR BIOGRAPHY

Daisy published her first novel, *The Mercies of Gwenda Wade*, at the tender age of 50. She is now concentrating on two follow up books and short stories for magazines while providing editorial support, sensitivity edits and writing sessions for charities in the UK. An obsession with sharing her love of writing & reading has encouraged the development of a new website. Launching at the beginning of 2024, both audio & signing will be available for the golden age stories she writes. Daisy has lived in the UAE since 2010 where she is an active member of the literary scene.

Crescents are Perfect

By Rohini Sunderam

◆◆◆◆

The whistling whisper of Fatima's sigh awoke the memory of that scene so fresh yet two years old in its sepia-toned sadness. Sitting wordless, at her mother's bedside holding her hand. Squeezing it as gently as she could, while her mind screamed "don't let go, if you hold on, she'll be forced back to life."

Mama opened her eyes briefly, looked straight at her, smiled her hint of a crescent moon smile. A tiny nod and she was gone.

"Two years, six months and two weeks." Fatima muttered, her arms were mechanical, placing each piece of baklava on the trays for the evening's Ramadan offering. "I can't carry on. I can't go to that empty, mindless chattering party tonight. I'll just send the sweets!" The vehemence of her thoughts was at odds with the delicate, practiced care, with which she arranged the sweets. Neat little rows, each brown, nut-filled confection, sticky with sugar syrup.

That first year after her mother's death had floated by; it was a mirage in the heat of her loss. And then Tariq died in that bizarre manner, out on the desert. There was always another memory that nudged her, one that she'd push away because, if she tried to look at it, the air became so thin she felt couldn't breathe, her chest tightened, and her hands would twitch.

The *halwa,* featureless as the dunes in the Rub al Khali, nestled on the tray. The tiny sweet *samboosas.* That was the true desert. The wasteland of Saudi Arabia where only the Bedouin survived. The trays were ready, and the foil neatly wrapped around them. That was her life now. She remembered something else, an odd fragment, a crescent dune, and a roadside. She shivered.

In Bahrain, Fatima had never experienced the kind of heat she'd known as a girl of five. It was thirty years since they'd settled on the island and there was hardly any desert here. Not like that. There was nothing like that. The wild undulating sands packed hard in some places, in others soft, shifting sands susurrating as the winds stirred them. Now, after losing her mother, and her husband, one after the other, Fatima's heart had become as hard and dry as the desert of the Rub al Khali. The blistering anger that burned behind her calm exterior had dried out her tears. Sometimes when contemplating her inner emptiness, she saw mirages in her mind as real as those she'd experienced on the open desert when they drove from Dammam to Hofuf and then Najran.

On those trips, her father was transformed into another being, a Bedouin of old. He'd chant the ancient stories to Fatima and her brother Mohammed. The two of them were mesmerised, not so much by the stories as the raw, hard, melodious burr of their father's voice. Conjuring up Arab horses running wild across the dunes, or djinns and *ghoulas* wailing through the sands. Sitting in the back seat of the car, Fatima thought she saw their wild hair and hands beckoning to her in the distance. She'd silently will her father to drive faster and faster. The only link to the comfort of the SUV and reality had been her mother's half-amused smile and gentle eyes as she looked at her children through the rear-view mirror on the passenger's side. Sometimes Fatima would catch her mother's amused look and flash her a smile back. But her Baba's voice had held a fascination of a different kind and soon she'd be drawn back into his stories, back to the dunes and the djinns.

Eventually those trips had tapered off in their frequency and the family decided to stay in Bahrain. School. Growing up. Another blur as empty and devoid of any life-giving memory as the sand-swept road to Najran.

It seemed as if it was only after she'd finished school that her family life began to fill with memories and moments. Before that it was school and friends. Learning things. Being punished. College. The International Business degree she'd earned. The thrill that coursed through her when her mother hugged her tight, tears brimming with pride on the edge of her eyes. Her father too had been pleased. A mere grunt and smile of pleasure. His black eyes shining jet in the light of the auditorium.

Then she met Tariq, introduced by her father's cousin and all her plans for joining a company or getting involved in Baba's business flew out of the window. It was an unexpected *shamal*, a wind that swept everything else away. Tariq, like her father, belonged to, what Fatima saw as a "wild" Saudi clan. At first, she'd been nervous of him. He too had a voice that was rich with stories of the past. His eyes dark as onyx and sometimes as inscrutable, edged with laugh lines that crinkled at the slightest amusement. Mama reassured her with a smile, "They're as caring as they are passionate, child," she had said, assuring Fatima that all would be well.

It had been, for all of four months. And then the occasional slap, developed into full-on punches. She covered up the bruises behind her *abaya* or with skilful make-up. Some nights Tariq would come home, and he'd be quiet. She'd lie next to him her body curled into a taut foetal position until she could hear him snore. Then she relaxed and slept.

Other nights he'd have his dinner and talk to her his voice lulling her into a sense of normalcy. And then the strangest little things would set him off. Some days there wasn't enough salt in the food. The saltshaker would be sent flying in a fit of rage. If she dodged it, a slap would follow. It was crazy things. And it was always at night.

She had shared none of this with her mother. The cancer that had shown up after her father died had robbed Mama of all the sparkle that was left in her eyes. Occasionally her crescent of a smile would light up her face.

"*Habibti*, is everything ok with you and Tariq?"

"Hmmm." Fatima smiled not saying anything more.

"No babies, yet? It's almost three years, la? Maybe you should see a doctor?"

"I will, just get well and I will, I promise you." And Fatima never let that line of conversation go any further.

Mohammed got married as he'd promised their mother he would, before the cancer became worse.

Then Mama joined Baba in the life beyond, if indeed there was a life beyond.

Last year – just as she was getting out of the mind-deadening depression from losing Mama – Tariq decided to take her on that old road, the one she had once travelled with her parents and her brother. They were to drive across the causeway to Dammam and from there they planned to go to Hofuf and then Najran. She laughed for the first time in years. "My parents used to take us on that exact same route," she told him.

"We'll camp en route," he said.

"Why? There are hotels!"

"It might help." He had smiled. "My doctor thinks I need to do something different, connect with my roots or something, to alleviate the night headaches and…" he gave her a lop-sided grin. "I'm sorry for the uncontrolled…" he didn't finish what he was saying.

"You've been seeing a doctor?" Fatima was surprised.

"Yes, I think, there's something wrong. And he's given me medicines but … he thinks this may help too."

Ramu, the servant, packed the tent and sleeping bags, the cooler with water and the food she'd ordered to take along with two vacuum flasks – one coffee, one hot water for tea – into the back of the SUV.

The journey to Dammam was bland, uninteresting, and over before one knew it. On the road to Hofuf, Fatima kept getting tearful at the memories the journey brought back.

"It's time you stopped crying about it." Tariq's voice took on the low ominous growl that Fatima had begun to recognise as an early warning sign. Next, he launched into his usual diatribe. "You're wallowing in your grief. It's as though you don't want to let go of it. Everyone must see what a martyr you are to your poor sick mother!"

"Tariq!" She shouted back. It was the first time she'd raised her voice at him. "Leave it! I *am* still grieving for her. Baba's passing, I somehow managed. But Mama was my life. I feel as if I have lost a limb. I can't focus, I can't think, I can't carry on!"

"Well, you had better," he yelled back at her. And then he went into one of his sullen silences. His hands gripped the steering wheel like it was her throat. The look on his face turned hard as the packed sand of a *barchan* dune. Fatima compressed her own lips into an equally hard fixed crescent, albeit a downturned one. They drove on for almost one hundred and fifty kilometres in silence.

As they approached an open area without much vegetation but with firm sand and a secluded spot beyond a crescent shaped dune, he screeched the vehicle to a halt.

"We'll camp here," Tariq announced.

"You still want to camp? I don't think this is going to work."

He remained silent and set up the tent.

She busied herself with setting out the food, it was cold stuff, hummus and mutabbel, stuffed vine leaves, pita, cooked kibbe, falafel. The only hot things were the tea water and coffee. "We could have brought the cook and a stove," she mumbled.

"I wanted us to be alone," he said.

"It's not exactly working out, is it?" Her tone was dry yet laced with bitterness.

"It had better, everyone's asking about why we haven't started a family yet, and I thought, I had hoped, that here, under the stars and in the quiet privacy of our old traditions you might be moved."

"*I* might be moved?" she was incredulous. "I thought this was your doctor's orders!" The words had barely left her lips when she regretted it. She closed her eyes fully expecting a backhanded slap to land on her face. It didn't come. When she opened her eyes, he was clutching the ends of his *guthra*.

After a very long moment, his lips a straight hard line clamped tight over his lips, he whispered, "I'm sorry. I'm trying. I want us to work."

His voice almost calmed her, and she might have allowed herself to relax if he hadn't continued, then in a rasping voice, his lips curled, he hissed, "Instead, you want to carry on with this excessive grieving. *My Mama is my life!* I mean it's over a year, dammit! You need to snap out of it. It's unhealthy. You need to see a doctor, a psychiatrist..." His soft, deep voice began to sound like a menacing djinn released from the dune behind them. It sent a chill ripple up her spine. Every nerve in her body was suddenly strung tight as the strings on an *oudh*.

The last thing she heard was, "I need to get you, to have you ..."

She had screamed. He *was* a djinn. He was dark, his hair was standing on end, his mouth was a gaping hole. His eyes had turned red. He was coming towards her. Reaching out to grab her.

"No! no! no," she screamed, her voice high-pitched like a *ghoula*. She was a *ghoula*, she had the strength of one of those spirit beings of the sand. Tonight, she was not going to give in. The deep Mother Desert reached into her depths and gave Fatima the strength she had needed all these years. Her eyes narrowed. She held a paring knife that had been packed along with the paper napkins, tight in her hand. She could feel it's comforting handle firm against her palm, "Stay away from me! Don't come any closer," she hissed.

He didn't see the knife. She lunged at him burying the sharp little blade deep into his neck. She pulled it out and stabbed again and again. He was a djinn. He was a djinn. He was a djinn. Baba drive faster, faster, faster. Babaaaaaaa!

She passed out. When she awoke it was a searing hot morning.

Tariq lay next to her covered in blood. Dead. Had she killed him? She looked at her hands. Nothing. Clean and pure as a wind-washed sand dune. There was no knife. What had happened! She ran to the car sick and crying. She desperately dialled her brother's number, "Tariq, Tariq..." she sobbed almost incoherent.

"What is it, Fatima? You're not making sense." Mohammed had shouted back, "What did that shit of a man do?"

Somehow between gagging sobs and screams, she told him where she was and that when she'd woken up Tariq was dead. Covered in blood. And there was no sign of any intruder that she could make out.

The rest was a blur. A posse of police turned up along with her brother. They asked her a whole lot of questions.

"Nothing, nothing, nothing," she had screamed and cried. But she said nothing about the djinn and the *ghoula* and nothing about the knife. Where was the knife?

Mohammed begged the officers to let his sister recover before they asked her any more questions. "She has been under a lot of stress since my mother's illness and death," he explained.

"It looks like there are stab marks in the man's throat." One of the cops said to him. "But there is no sign of any weapon or knife."

"Make your searches," Mohammed said, "Keep the vehicle if you must, but please let me take my sister back to Bahrain."

They took her fingerprints and rapidly ran a metal detector over her abaya that revealed nothing other than the usual beeps for jewellery and underwear. Mohammed handed over his credit card details for bail, he shepherded her into his vehicle, and they drove back to Bahrain.

"What did that tyrant of a man do?"

"You knew?"

"I suspected, something sister, but you never said anything. I wouldn't blame you if you did. Did you?"

Fatima just shook her head, her body swaying in that old rhythm of grief.

"Something just isn't right," said Reem, a newly appointed Wakil Raqib – Detective Sergeant – in the Eastern Province of the Kingdom's police force. Reem had been a student and admirer of Saudi Arabia's first female detective, Nadeen Alsayat; Fatima was her first woman suspect in a murder case. "These look like knife marks."

"He was her husband," interjected Sergeant Major Rais Ruquba Jameel.

"There is a lot of domestic violence, even in our dear sweet neighbour, Bahrain," Reem smiled, her eyes crinkling.

"But there's no sign of a struggle," Jameel insisted. "They come from a respected family!"

Reem smiled some more, "Aeyi, respected!" she rolled her eyes, and her smile grew wider and more noticeable even behind her veil, "But you're right. No struggle and so much blood. The killer went straight for the jugular." She paced around the tent with Jameel following close behind. "Also, no footprints either entering or leaving the tent. I know. That could easily be the wind." She took out her phone and began taking photographs.

"The team has already taken photos of everything."

"I like to have my own," Reem said. "Tell me again, why did we let her go?"

"They're from a well-known family, in construction, his family, the victim's family, are Saudi. We called them, they said they weren't pressing any charges until we investigate further. She won't run, she can't."

"I'll need to go and talk to her soon." Reem looked at her superior, her eyes hard. "While things are still fresh."

Two weeks later the two women met at a quiet place in the lobby of a hotel. Fatima's brother, Mohammed sat apart from them.

"You must understand, madam," Reem's voice was soft as the gentle tides of the Arabian Gulf, "if we are to find the perpetrator of this horrible crime you must give me more information other than that you woke up and saw him covered in blood."

Fatima shook her head slowly from side to side, her eyes wide with fear, "Yes. Yes. I understand but no, no, there was no one else there. Maybe he went out? Maybe an intruder? I don't know."

"And you slept through it all?"

"There is no other explanation. You think I killed my husband? Why? Why? Why?" Fatima's voice rose shrill as the wind as it whistles around the dunes.

"Hush, madam, hush. Please don't shout. I don't want to take you to a police station for questioning, I'm just trying to get a better picture."

Fatima's voice dropped down to a conspiratorial whisper, "Maybe it was the desert djinn, have you considered that?" And then she clamped her teeth, went silent, and continued rocking back and forth.

Reem could get nothing more out of her after that.

After another two weeks, she visited Fatima's house, a beautiful, large villa in Riffa.

She questioned the servants at Fatima's home. Asked about any signs of domestic violence. They said nothing. Reem spoke to Fatima's brother again asked carefully whether there had been any case of violence reported.

"Reported?" Mohammed asked. "No. Never. You know how it is, our women don't consider the occasional slap, violence, and abuse. It's not like in the West."

"You're right," Reem replied. "But, still, it is time these things changed. *Sah?*"

"Right."

Then she tentatively asked Mohammed if Fatima had visited a grief counsellor.

"We have no history of mental illness in our family," he almost snapped at her.

"Sir, please understand, we are trying to solve a murder case," Reem spoke as she always did in a soft voice. "And a history of mental illness doesn't apply in this case. Your sister has been under extended stress, what with taking care of your mother and then losing her, and then this bizarre 'accident' shall we say?"

"Yes."

That was last year. Now they were into Ramadan and Fatima had been making the sweets to share with the neighbours. She had continued to live in her home after Tariq's death. His clothes still hung in the cupboard. She had left them there more out of inertia than any feelings for him. For the most part she was lighter and happier than she'd ever been.

This evening that woman cop from Saudi was coming again.

Arabian Noir

Why didn't she just give up! Stupid, persistent thing. And why come during Ramadan! Wasn't she fasting? Besides which, after all this time, surely, she, herself, wasn't a suspect anymore. Fatima's own crescent moon smile flashed across her face for an instant.

The doorbell rang.

"Ramu!" Fatima called the watchman-cum-general help.

"Yes, madam! I'm opening the door."

It was Mohammed's driver who had come to collect the sweets. After Ramu loaded them into the car he asked Fatima if she needed him for anything else.

"Not just now," Fatima said, "but remind Mary that the police lady from Saudi will be coming at seven, and we'll need tea, coffee, and some dates, *ma'amoul*, sweets."

Then she sat and waited in the fading light. Other than Mary the cook waiting quietly in the kitchen everyone else had left. She broke her fast in solitary peace, surveying the table and enjoying the quietude of an empty house, she sat motionless at the table for a long time. Memories like dust eddies, swirled through her mind, her mother's strong comforting embrace, her brother's laughter, her father's twinkling eyes and encouraging nods when she did well at school. The house grew dark around her. She jumped up and put on a few lights.

The doorbell rang.

"She's here." Fatima steeled her nerves and sat in her chair with her hands together. when Wakil Raqib Reem entered the room, Fatima remained seated. "*Aahlen*," she smiled and indicated a chair to her left.

Reem sat down carefully placing her cap on a small ornate gilt-edged side table and slowly removed her veil. "*Ramadan kareem*," she greeted her hostess.

"*Ramadan kareem*," Fatima responded. She rang a little bell and Mary wheeled in a trolley. The two women exchanged the standard pleasantries, enquiring about each other's families while the maid set out the tea and cakes.

When they were alone again, Fatima asked, "Have you made any progress in your enquiries? I mean you're here to see me about that, aren't you?"

"Unfortunately, madam you are still the primary suspect."

"You still have our vehicle and the food hamper, surely they must have revealed something, if I were still suspected."

"We will be bringing the vehicle and its contents back," Reem assured her. "And yes, there are a couple of things that aren't clear to me. You and your husband hadn't eaten anything. The food was still set out in front of the tent. But the flask with the hot water was empty."

"What does that mean?"

"Madam, a lawyer could allege that you washed your hands and that's why there was no blood on your hands and no water in the flask."

"But there was no weapon, right? And there was no blood on me!"

"Yes, madam. But an *abaya* could be changed. And, you're right madam, we have still not found anything that could have been a weapon. From the wounds it appears that it was a short-bladed knife that went straight into the jugular and several stab marks, all in the front of the neck."

"But the food was all cooked, and cold; we didn't need a knife,"

Fatima started to get that glazed look on her face.

Reem knew that once she went there, all coherence would be lost. "Madam, madam, please relax. Have some tea. Please. Why don't you have some *ma'amoul*."

"Forgive me," Fatima's expression came back to normal. "Please help yourself. The *ma'amoul* is very good. The dates are from my brother's garden."

Reem took a deep breath. She had enlarged one of her own photographs and seen a depression in the sand on Fatima's side of the tent. It could have been caused by water being poured, to wash hands, face? She asked her again. "You keep mentioning a djinn. Did you see a djinn?"

Fatima rolled her eyes. "I see djinns often. Even here."

Reem whispered, "Did your husband ever strike you, hit you?"

Fatima raised a finger to her lips, "Shhhh. The djinn will hear you, maybe he will come to get you. Don't disregard the ancient stories. Or even the modern ones." Her voice suddenly turned normal.

"How do you mean, the modern ones?"

"You know what they say in all the detective stories, the criminal always returns to the scene of the crime."

"Yes, madam. That is true. We have set up a hidden camera there." She bit her tongue. How could she have been so careless as to reveal that to this woman, the one and only suspect in this case.

"Ohhh. That is good. That is clever. And is it true? That the perpetrator always returns?"

"Most of the time. You see they usually do leave a clue that will show up sometimes even years later."

"Hmmmm?" Fatima stared into the distance.

"Are you sure there isn't anything you want to tell me madam?

"No, no. I don't think so. We're finished for tonight, aren't we?"

Reem stood up, "I'll let you know if we learn anything new."

"Yes, please." Fatima didn't get up from her chair; she rang her bell and Mary came in. "Please..." she indicated that Mary should lead Reem out of the house.

Fatima sat in her chair for a long while after the policewoman left. Memories whirled like dervishes in her brain.

A djinn with his gaping mouth and wild hair. Beatings and slaps. A knife with a small crescent blade not more than six centimetres. A blood-spattered *abaya*. A wild-haired *ghoula* desperately pushing, pushing, pushing it into the base of a dune, a crescent dune.

And then the hot water. Her hands and arms clean, unblemished as wind-washed sand. Followed by a dreamless sleep.

Finally, Fatima got up from her chair and walked slowly and silently up the stairs of her enormous house to her bedroom.

But where was the knife?

There was no memory there. And now that she knew there was a camera planted near the place, she was never going back there to check. Never, ever.

She went into her bathroom and opened the vanity cabinet above the washbasin. There among her toiletries was her packet of sanitary pads: always.

She closed the cabinet door, looked in the mirror and remembered. The knife sandwiched between two sanitary pads and worn.

Behind her own perfect crescent smile and bright eyes for a brief moment she saw a *ghoula*.

AUTHOR BIOGRAPHY

Rohini Sunderam is a semi-retired advertising copywriter. She has written two books as commissioned assignments, had articles published in The Statesman, Calcutta, India, The Globe & Mail, Canada, and The Halifax Chronicle Herald, Nova Scotia, Canada. Rohini is the author of *Corpoetry*, a collection of light-hearted verse about corporate life and *Desert Flower*, (as Zohra Saeed) a romantic story set in 1930s Bahrain, both published by *Ex-L-Ence* publishing, UK. You can find out more about her at: https://bwcbh.com/welcome/rohini-sunderam/

The Thing About Maryam

By Mohanalakshmi Rajakumar

◆◆◆◆

Blood spread across the marble of the kitchen floor like a slow creeping stain. The woman's life force had surged out from her with the same gusto in which she lived – judging by the photos crowded on the front of the fridge.

Ali wiped sweat from his brow. Normally he didn't get involved in suicides. Not since his reinstatement to Qatar's elite intelligence unit, anyway. But normally expat women didn't fall over in their kitchens with their wrists slashed either. Even this wouldn't be enough to warrant Ali's attention.

"Why, why, why – " the husband's wail came from the living room. "She was in remission. She was doing so well. She was over that depression stuff."

The laments, worse than anything Ali had heard, were cut off by his partner closing the kitchen door. Now the air took on a sticky sweetness that Ali couldn't stomach for long. But he was glad for the silence.

"Boss." Manu flipped up the edge of the woman's shirt. Ten stab wounds dotted the torso. "More."

Ali ran his palms under the water. Death, blood, murder, mayhem – he trained for all of these things. But ever since he got married, the violence against women hit him differently.

"Why would she kill herself!"

Ali's mobile buzzed jolting him from the crescendo in the other room.

"*Salaam Alikum.*"

"*Alikum a salaam,*" Fahad's voice was gritty from a sleepless night. "So, what's the story. Local unit says the husband did it."

Ali forced himself to glance at the prone body again. "Could be. Multiple stab wounds."

Manu mouthed 'forty.' Mercifully a sheet now covered the woman's face.

"Crime of passion, okay, great. Done. Get him into custody."

"And take him to jail?"

Fahad exhaled. Ali stared at a spot in the ceiling, the same thoughts circling through his head.

"Ambassador's husband? In a regular prison." The silence stretched between them.

"So, you want me to –"

Dawn crept into the kitchen window sending long fingers of sunlight across the counter.

"Bring him in. Find an excuse. Now I have more people to wake up."

The line went dead. Manu worked the scene, calmly, and thoroughly, taking photos of the body and scribbling away in a notebook. In the matter of a few years, they had completely switched roles. Ali was the one who used to pass him a paper bag at the first sign of rigor mortis while he did the crime detail. When he had to prove his worth, despite what the medical report said, that he was half a man, Manu was all he had to rely on.

With a slap, the kitchen door burst open, hitting the wall. Hair on end, looking more ghost than human, the husband stared at the prone body. Tears coursed down his face in an unstoppable tide.

All for show Ali thought in disgust. *May God have mercy on him.*

"Mr. Meyer, please, we are needing you to stay out of here." Manu gently steered the much bigger man back towards the living room.

"My wife – my wife."

At those words, Ali snapped back to attention. "Mr. Meyer, you are right. You shouldn't stay in here. Let me take you down to my office so you can tell me again what happened."

Small, medium, large. They were like three specimens of the range of humanity, Manu, Meyer, and Ali. What seemed like muscled resistance became like softened *halloumi* in Ali's firm grip. He had the man by the elbow and out into the hallway before Meyer could make a sound. At seven a.m. the street in front of the villa was awash in the normalcy of daylight. Ali slung himself into the SUV and the shaken Meyer did the same. Dark circles were puddles under his eyes, the skin pasty now, with tears and lack of sleep.

Small talk. Oh shi – the bleat of the phone through the Bluetooth broke through the stretching silence.

"So, we're not going to breakfast?"

Despite the grit and horror of the evening, and the presence of a murderer in his vehicle. Ali smiled. Even in the darkest of night, Maryam was the steadiest of suns.

"Maybe I can make it brunch."

Meyer let out a yelp. Too much normalcy. He pressed against the door as if it was one of those airplane life rafts.

If only all he had to do was survive a plane crash. Ali reached behind the seat to hand over a tissue box. *The storm ahead of him is far worse.*

"Okay. Brunch it is then. See you."

"See you."

And they were ensconced in silence again. Ali pressed the accelerator, eager to be rid of his unwanted charge.

Resplendent in a gold trim *abaya*, her *shayla* draped halfway on her head, Maryam waited for her husband. He was only forty minutes behind. For Ali, this was close to being on time. She drank another cup of tea, trying to let the taste of ginger soothe her nerves. This was no ordinary morning – waking up to find Ali missing had been just the start of it. His job as an intelligence officer kept him closer to home which she preferred since their last caper, the one that saw them married, and also breaking up an international terrorist cell, had cost them the life of her childhood friend Sharif.

"Shall I bring the food Madam?" The petite Filipina waitress asked for the third time.

"No, the food will get cold." Maryam adjusted the printout she slipped in the breadbasket.

"More hot water?"

"What – no, yes, fine. Yes."

The waitress scurried away, happy to be given a task. In the near empty restaurant, Maryam stood out like a child's forgotten marble. Since all the other staff were scrolling on their phones, she took hers out to avoid their covert sympathetic glances. Daniel's text was a like a bolt of electricity.

Something is going on at the British Embassy. Lots of police. Would Ali know anything?

Maryam sat up, now on full alert. She texted back: *Tell me any other details.*

Their nascent reporting site, Corniche News, was being tolerated by everyone – including the government who kept a tight lid on the media, like all countries in the region. But Maryam managed to get in a few things outside of the usual events related press releases. Ali swore he couldn't help them. And tried to be as tight lipped as possible but if she got the jump by catching him off guard ...

Someone crossed a line. Big one. At least twenty cars outside. All appointments cancelled for the rest of the week. No one in since the morning.

"You have a reservation sir?" Ali ignored the manager and strode straight towards her.

Maryam willed herself to stay seated though the sight of him, broad shoulders, long strides in his *thobe* made her light up. Jumping to greet him would start them off on the wrong foot. He would be flustered by the attention, and aware of the watching eyes on the young local couple and tense up before the meal had a chance to begin. She waited in her seat, soft as the butter on the table.

"*Salaam*," he said gruffly as the waitress came back to hover at his elbow.

"Now you can bring it," Maryam said.

The waitress nodded.

"*Salaam*," she said. His skin had a greyish tinge. "You, okay?"

Ali gulped a glass of water before replying.

"Was it someone at the British Embassy who died, or did they kill someone?"

Ali choked on his water. She passed him a napkin.

"I won't ask how you knew that."

"What can you tell me?"

He grabbed at the breadbasket as a distraction. "Right when you need someone," he looked around for the wait staff who were all nowhere to be seen. "They're all busy."

She held her breath, the line of questioning paused, as he grabbed at the paper.

"Such low hygienic standards – "Ali's voice faded away. "What is this?" He enunciated each word. The black and white square image shook in his grasp.

"That, husband," she said. "Is the first image of our baby."

He drank again, convulsively. This time Maryam covered his hand, where it shook on the table and stilled it with her own. "It shouldn't be possible, but it is." They had only spoken of Ali's deformity once, caused by a childhood fever, that cost him a testicle and almost his career. In their conversative, family-oriented society, marriage and fatherhood had always been off the table for him.

"Someone killed the British Ambassador."

Maryam clamped down on his hand. He gripped it in return. "Someone?"

"The husband."

Reflexively she let go, his fingers still reaching for her. "The husband."

The waitress came with dishes loaded with beans, eggs, and beef bacon. She placed them on the table as Maryam regarded Ali with consternation. Neither made a move towards the food.

"It's not surprising. Most of the violence committed against women is by someone they know. Someone they know well."

"I know that, thanks Cosmo."

"Who's she?"

"Never mind. Tell me more."

Ali tore a piece of bread into smaller and smaller pieces. "You can't write about this," he warned.

She spread her hands, the picture of innocence. "I deserve to know what pulled my husband out of bed in the middle of the night." Maryam buttered a piece of toast. "And what will keep him away from his children."

Ali's eyes narrowed at her. "She had been out late, a friend dropped her off, the husband came in and called 999 when he saw the body."

"They had both been drinking?"

He shook his head. "We're not doing this."

"What he called 999 and confessed to murdering a diplomat on foreign soil because – she – cheated? Or what do expats fight about?"

He pointed at her. "Too much Kardashians."

"If you want to insult my intelligence, please first tell me why I've made you angry." Maryam pouted. "But also, I didn't think you knew who they were."

Ali cracked a smile. "Even I get bored sometimes." He chewed thoughtfully. "Blood report isn't back. Who knows what was in either of their systems. But he wasn't there at the time of the stabbing. He was at a friend's. They have CCTV of him entering and leaving the apartment."

"But husbands are murderers so…"

"You didn't hear the 999 call." He waved no to the question before she could even ask. "No. You cannot. But it sounded so fake. Over the top."

"Hm...."

"Hmm, tell me more about – about – this," he stumbled and touched the ultrasound image again. "How long have you known?"

"I'm just saying, if you're not looking at the last person who saw her alive, then, I have a few podcasts I can recommend."

"Maryam," Ali growled.

"Six weeks."

"Six!"

She buttered her toast with a smile. "See, women can keep secrets. Who knows which ones the ambassador was hiding."

Ali scanned the reports for what felt like the umpteenth time. Since the World Cup, the diligence at the airport had been stepped up. Human trafficking, money laundering, drugs – all of it was looking for a safe onward journey though one of the Middle East's biggest hubs. Weeks of this and they managed to flag one mother traveling with two children who had a suitcase full of pork; a group of guys trying to hide poker chips across a bunch of bags, and some highschoolers with contraband wine from a school spring break trip. All he was missing were a few Playboy magazines for his junior detective starter kit.

"Sir, that man, they will deport him for killing the ambassador," said Manu.

Ali snapped out of the haze of suitcase scans, flight landing details and passenger manifests.

"The Meyer guy?"

Manu nodded. He passed over the newspaper. A photo on the front showed a man in handcuffs, a sweater over his head, being led into court.

"Wow, they printed that."

"Big news sir. All over the world." Manu nudged his elbow to the bank of television screens on the opposite wall. Some were for internal security cameras and others were for news channels from around the world. Most of the European ones were flashing the same image from the paper as well as the couple in happier times. He grabbed the remote and turned up the volume on the middle one, where a woman in a pink sweater was talking with a well-manicured reporter.

"This must be so hard for you," the immaculate reporter said with just the right touch of empathy.

"She was my best friend," the woman agreed in a crisp British accent.

She's a bit old for that. Ali heard Maryam in his ear. The first few times this happened to him, he was shocked. Worried that he had become one of those men who were tied to their homes by over interference. But he'd come to rely on this new aspect. What he saw as another side of himself. One that was more intuitive and caught details he sometimes missed.

"Take us back to the night, when you last saw her. If you're allowed to talk about it. We understand the case is still open." Again, with the measured sympathy. This guy was so good he could have been an actor playing a reporter.

"Yes, of course." With a measured laugh. "I'm not a suspect." She fingered the pennant dangling from her necklace.

Not yet. Ali groaned inwardly. He couldn't go to Fahad with his wife's theories and a hunch about the woman's body language.

"Manu."

"Huh."

"Get me everything you can on the woman."

Manu turned to him in confusion. "Which woman sir?"

Ali sighed. He pinched the bridge of his nose. Because once these words were said, they would put into play a whole chain of actions that couldn't be undone. A chain that would go all the way up to the top of the leadership of two governments, given how profile the relationship between them was, and the nature of the person who had been murdered.

"The best friend," Ali said. "Let's see where she was after the drop off."

AUTHOR BIOGRAPHY

Mohanalakshmi Rajakumar is a South Asian American writer, with a PhD in English, who also moonlights as a stand-up comic. In her routines and writing, audiences experience what it means to be brown and female in a supposedly post-racial era. Mohana creates humorous feminist and cultural content. In her solo show *Being Brown is My Superpower*, she channels a lifetime of cultural misunderstandings, has been accepted at the Edinburgh Fringe and United Solo Festivals. Most recently she has been working on a crime novel featuring an Arab detective. You can find out more at: https://mohadoha.com

Footnote

By Glen R Stansfield

◆◆◆◆

1966

'Members of the jury, I have your note indicating that you have reached a verdict. Will the Clerk of the Court please take the verdict?'

'Mr. Foreman, has the jury agreed upon a verdict?'

'They have.'

'As to the count of murder in the first degree what is the jury's verdict?'

'Guilty!'

Three Months Earlier

Martha stared into the distance, a frequent occurrence these days. The wide expanse of wheat rippled gently in the summer breeze. Some folks said the golden yellow of the plants reminded them of a sea of sand, or a desert. As someone who'd not been to neither she had no idea. Perhaps one day if she got rich, she'd take a trip and seem em both. Next week, a huge combine harvester would begin consuming the golden yellow plants; an insatiable mechanical beast — not theirs of course, but one rented by the local farmers for the harvest.

Harvest for her was a bitter-sweet time of the year. Gone would be the golden dancers, replaced by a field devoid of all beauty, but it meant money in the bank and heaven knows how much she needed that.

The screen door slammed shut. She sighed out loud and mentally started the count.

'Martha — MARTHA.'

She only reached four, not a good sign.

Where did it all go wrong?

To use the term rural town would confer a certain status which Rattlebone, Montana, consistently struggled to achieve.

Apart from a paved road and electric street lighting, the only discernible difference between the current town, and the one of the nineteenth century, the farm hands no longer tied their steeds to the rail outside the saloon. Had there still been a rail, they probably would have tied their trucks to it. The nineteen-sixties hadn't quite reached this farming community — the rest of the world had been there some six years.

Yet the hustle and bustle of modern American life remained absent here. People still found time to stop and chat. Townsfolk all knew each other and of course, many of the farmers in the surrounding district.

Jimmy and Martha Ellis were no exception, although if challenged, people would find it hard to remember the last time they'd seen Jimmy in his beat-up drop-side pickup truck. Most didn't care. Jimmy had become a bitter, twisted, and cantankerous man over the years.

Martha however, remained the same sweet soul she had always been, even if her shoulders seemed to stoop lower with every passing week.

While the town hadn't quite moved out of the nineteen-fifties, Dean's Emporium appeared firmly ensconced in the nineteenth century. Born long before city department stores, the general store was the original one-stop shop, from food to finery, boots to bullets. The proprietor of this particular store added to the illusion with his old-fashioned apron, round rimmed glassed, salt and pepper hair and handlebar moustache.

Henry Dean Junior was reading his latest edition of National Geographic Magazine, his sole indulgence. He was paying particular attention to a photo-feature on the Arabian Gulf. He longed to travel and because he couldn't do this in person, he did it on the page. The bell above the door sounded, he looked, and his heart fluttered when he spotted Martha Ellis enter the store. His facial muscles barely registered a twitch, and as the customer's change left his hands, the smile never left his face. Daddy taught him always to smile, keep eye contact, and the customer was always right, even when clearly wrong. The latter troubled him, but no doubt, a happy customer is a returning customer. Perhaps that's why the general store was still going strong. That, and the fact no right-minded chain store would invest in what amounted to little more than a handful of houses at a crossroads.

'Martha, what a pleasure to see you again so soon.'

Although Henry spurned Martha's advances in his youth, over the years he realised his error and his desire for her grew. What she saw in Jimmy now, he did not know and suggested on more than one occasion she could do well to leave her husband and join him in running the store, as scandalous as it would be.

With such feelings, smiling at her proved easy, but at times Henry felt that once he finished in the store, he would remove his smile and hang it on a hook ready for the next morning.

'Likewise, I'm sure, Henry.' Her eyes took in the magazine on the counter. "And where has National Geographic taken you this month?"

"The Arabian Gulf."

"Where?"

He explained but after a minute or so her eyes had become glassy and she said, "Very nice, I'm sure."

Henry put away the magazine, 'So, what can I do for you today, Martha?'

He already knew the answer, he wished she had come to see him but knew this was not the case. It was the same reason for her last visit and the one before. Jimmy Ellis wanted new boots. If he'd told her once he'd told her a hundred times, she couldn't try the boots on herself and gauge whether they would fit her husband.

Every two years they would have this discussion and always the outcome remained the same; several weeks toing and froing with different boots until Jimmy found a pair to his satisfaction, hence his inward groan when he saw her enter.

'I'm so sorry, Henry, but these boots just don't fit right on Jimmy. We need to try some more.'

Henry's smile remained firmly in place; his voice remaining steady.

'Martha, if I've said this once I've said it a hundred times, I need the correct pair of feet in the store. I don't know why Jimmy doesn't just come here himself.'

Of course, he was fully aware of why Jimmy didn't come to town, but surely, they should put all that behind them now.

1917

Two pairs of legs and a furry tail dangled from the fallen log which bridged the stream. Flies danced over the surface and the occasional splash punctuated the gentle gurgle of water as a trout found a tasty snack.

Two of the legs belonged to Jimmy. As an only child, a rarity in the farming community but one caused by his mother's medical condition, Jimmy did his fair share around the farm. So, he relished the times when he could get away to meet his friend at the creek, spending time with stick, string, hook and worm, pursuing trout. To Jimmy, nothing tasted better than freshly caught grilled trout.

The second pair of legs belonged to Henry, whose view of fish and the catching of them was somewhat different. He didn't like either that much, which is why he invariably gave his catch to Jimmy, that's if he ever caught anything. He would only bait his hook when Jimmy was looking. His reason for coming to the creek was the company. Even at his tender age he understood the value of friendship.

The tail, of course belonged to Jimmy's dog, Bobby, who had no interest in the fishing itself, only the fish.

Henry Dean Senior owned the only general store for many a mile and business was doing quite nicely thank you. Without competition, Dean's Emporium was making a tidy sum of money although this never reflected in the family lifestyle which remained simple almost to the point of being austere. The only two people who had knowledge of the family's true worth were Mr Dean and the manager of the local Wells Fargo bank.

Jimmy's father kept his head above water in the farming business and although the farm was mortgaged, it made enough profit to make the monthly payments and a little left over for them not to live hand to mouth.

Despite their vastly different backgrounds, the bond between them that started in kindergarten, grew stronger every year. It seemed the pair would spend their rest of their lives as friends, although they both realised Jimmy would have little time when he took over the farm.

1928

The highlight of the year for many of the farmers, farm hands and families in Rattlebone was the annual harvest dance. The event gave them an opportunity to let their hair down and have a rattling good time. Of course, in this era of prohibition the dance should be a muted affair but surprisingly, they were as rambunctious as those that went before.

Farms proved to be ideal places to build illicit stills and of course, most of the ingredients grew right out of the ground. With a town Deputy who was partial to a drop or two himself, prohibition in Rattlebone had little effect.

Things were in full swing when Martha Becker decided to make her move. As the daughter of a farmer, she could not see that as the life for her. She had her mind set on the finer things, the sort of things that could only come from money, and although there were few outward signs, there was no doubt where the money lay in this town.

Martha took a deep breath, time to put her plan into action. She crossed the room to where Henry Dean Junior and Jimmy Ellis stood watching the dancing. She couldn't help but notice what a fine figure of a man Jimmy had become, but Jimmy was a farmer. Still, he was handsome and strong.

Focus Martha, focus.

After exchanging pleasantries Martha made her move.

'Henry, would you care to dance with me?'

'No, Martha, I would not. You are still a young girl and in case you hadn't noticed, I am a fully grown man.'

Martha could feel the colour rising in her cheeks and the tears welling up in her eyes. The words hurt as surely as if he had beaten her with a stick.

She fled across the dance floor bumping into people along the way.

'Henry! That was uncalled for. Can't you see you've hurt the girl.'

'It's alright for you, you don't have to put up with her making eyes at you every time she comes into the store.'

'Well, it ain't right and I'm going to check on her.'

Jimmy stepped through the door and paused momentarily to adjust his eyes to the darkness, although he could have relied solely on his hearing to locate Martha as her sobbing could clearly be heard coming from behind the barn.

'Martha?'

'Go away. I don't want you coming here mocking me.'

'I didn't come here to mock you; I came to make sure you were alright.'

'Why?'

'Because what Henry did was wrong.'

Jimmy sat with his back to the barn next to Martha who was squatting down with her head in her hands.

'What's it to you?'

Jimmy thought about that for a moment.

'Well, Henry's my friend and I don't like what my friend did to you. Besides, I think he's wrong about you. Look at you, you're, getting all growed up Martha Becker. Why, I wouldn't mind that dance with you myself.'

Martha looked at Jimmy from under her eyelashes, her eyes red and puffy.

'You're just saying that.'

Jimmy grabbed her hand.

'We'll see about that, c'mon.'

Henry reflected on what Jimmy had said to him. Perhaps he had been mean, but then again, Jimmy hadn't seen how she was with him in the store. It just got too much for him, mooning her eyes and fluttering her eyelashes every time he looked in her direction.

He had to admit now that he was looking at her in a new light as she danced with Jimmy. She'd become a different Martha Becker on the dance floor, perhaps he had been hasty in turning her down. She was turning into quite a young lady.

1930

'Gentlemen, what we have on sale today is this prime farmland, a hundred and fifty acres turned over to potatoes and cereal crop, this fine homestead, farming equipment and livestock. As this is a foreclosure there are no reserves, so grab yourselves as many bargains as you like.'

Jimmy couldn't believe it. All this effort by him and his father to make the farm work and now the bank were foreclosing. In the past year they managed to create a marvellous seed potato crop. It looked like their foray into that side of growing would pay handsome dividends, but life doesn't always play fair.

No one but a few clever financiers could have forecast what would happen that day in nineteen-twenty-nine, but Tuesday October 29th affected millions of lives as billions of dollars were wiped off the value of shares on Wall Street. The knock-on effect was devastating.

People all over the USA found themselves unemployed as businesses failed one after the other and it wasn't just in industry this was felt. Rural areas were equally hit. As demand for produce fell, prices fell. Quite simply, people could no longer to afford to buy food and the entire economy was in freefall.

One year later, the bank wanted their money and Jimmy's father couldn't pay. They were barely surviving.

'Five cents for the plough.'

'Aww c'mon. Be serious.'

'Ima bein' serious. Five cents for the plough.'

Jimmy turned to the bidder, one of their close neighbours. Five cents? The plough was worth far more than that.

'Any advance on five cents?'

The auctioneer looked nervously at the crowd, but no one made eye contact, let alone bid. The auctioneer had no choice, with no reserves set and a bid made he would have to sell to the highest bidder.

'We all done here? Going once — going twice —.' He scanned the crowd hoping that someone would raise the bid. '— sold to the gentleman in the blue dungarees.'

That brought a few chuckles from the crowd. Nearly every one of them was wearing a pair of blue dungarees.

The winner turned to Jimmy and gave him a wink. In that moment, Jimmy realised what was happening and they would be okay. He'd heard about this sort of thing. It started in Nebraska and spread like wildfire amongst the farmers. The penny auction became a banker's nightmare.

Expecting to raise enough money to repay loans, the banks found themselves getting very little at the auctions. Other farmers refused to bid or would pay a few cents for equipment. This often resulted in the farm being bought back for just a handful of dollars and the equipment being handed back to the original owner.

And so, it was for the rest of the implements and livestock; a few cents bid on each item.

'Okay gentlemen, you've had your fun but let's get down to some serious business now. What am I bid for this prime land and homestead, and please, no one say fifty dollars?'

'Fifty-one dollars.'

Laughter broke out among the farmers and the auctioneer wiped the sweat from his brow.

'Sixty dollars.'

The crowd fell silent. No one was supposed to bid over the initial bid; they'd agreed that beforehand. Who the hell was breaking the unwritten rule?

Jimmy craned his neck to search out this new bidder then stared in disbelief. The father of his best friend, Henry Dean Senior, was going to buy out the farm from under them.

Jimmy's world stopped.

Although the farmers did their best to outbid Dean Senior, he won the auction with a bid of four-hundred-and-ninety-eight dollars.

Mr Dean Senior, having amassed a considerable amount of wealth from the emporium and hearing about the auction, decided that not only would he run a profitable store, but he would become a landlord and thus raise yet more income.

The fact he was willing to rent it back to Jimmy's father for a reasonable sum was irrelevant as far as Mr Ellis and the other farmers were concerned. What he had done was underhand and not in the spirit of the community, yet there was little to be done. Boycotting Dean's Emporium would cost them dearly, so they continued to buy from him, albeit with considerably less friendliness than before.

Naturally, Jimmy understood his father's anger at having the farm bought out from under him, but he felt he was going a step too far by vowing to never set foot in the store again. After all, they had little choice but to buy from the emporium, but his father was adamant he would not go, choosing to send Jimmy instead.

♦♦♦

It was Harvest Dance time again and heaven knew Jimmy needed this relief from the farm.

Ever since the auction, his father lost interest, not only in the farm but seemingly in life itself. His thoughts turned inward and whilst he did some work around the farm, he spent many a day in a drunken stupor. On more than one occasion he muttered to himself about double-crossing, back-stabbing bastards, bringing a rebuke from Jimmy's mother who, being a good and staunch Christian, would tolerate no cussing in her presence.

Many things had changed in Jimmy's life over this past year and a half. He rarely got to see Henry anymore. Whether that was because Henry was avoiding him since the incident over Martha or whether it was because Jimmy spent most of his spare time walking out with her, he wasn't sure, and quite frankly he didn't care. The more he thought about his relationship with Henry, the more he realised they had nothing in common.

Martha was another kettle of fish entirely. As young as she was, and although she'd said on more than one occasion that she'd no interest in farming, she proved to be knowledgeable about modern techniques, especially seed potato production.

Jimmy had reached the conclusion that he and Martha were a perfect match. Tonight would be the night to try to cement that relationship and that made Jimmy as nervous as a frog in a box with a rattlesnake.

What on earth was he doing?

Jimmy asked Martha to come and join him in front of the band.

'As most of you know, Martha and I have been walking out together for the past two years.'

A few murmurs of acknowledgment came from the room.

'Well, some of you will also know that today is Martha's eighteenth birthday.'

A chorus of cheers and happy birthdays ensued this time.

So that's what it was all about. He'd arranged a birthday surprise for her. She wondered what he had in mind. Then her eyes opened wide. Jimmy Ellis was down on one knee in front of her.

Through the thumping of her heart and the sound of blood rushing through her ears she heard him say,

'Martha Becker, will you do me the honour of becoming my wife?'

Her hands flew to her mouth, and she let out a small scream. The room fell silent. Everyone held their breath.

'Yes—Yes—YES!'

Martha threw her arms around him as the room erupted into a cacophony of hollering and whooping.

Despite Martha's certainty in the past that she didn't want to be a farmer's wife, something happened in her life that she had no knowledge of when she'd made that decision all those years ago.

Well, two things really. Henry Dean Junior had spurned her advances and she discovered Jimmy Ellis to be a wonderful lover. There weren't many occasions when they managed to be alone, and although still under the age of consent, she had willing given it. Actually, consent would be the wrong word, she instigated things with Jimmy as he had been the reluctant party, at first anyway.

Now she was eighteen, she could legally give that consent and to hell with the morality of it, not that the morals had ever been a concern to her. The church had its place, and it wasn't with them in the haystack.

1933

A homicide-suicide is what the police were calling it. No child should lose their parents in this way and no wife should ever have to stumble across such a sight.

Jimmy had been working in the fields when Martha went to town in the old truck to pick up supplies. When she returned, she told police she found Jimmy's father in his chair with the top of his head missing and Jimmy's mother in the garden where she'd been hanging out the washing. The back of her head blasted with a shotgun.

As much as Jimmy despised his father for taking to drink and generally letting himself go, he was still his father and that bond between father and son remained strong.

It took all of Martha's powers of persuasion and those of the Sheriff to stop Jimmy from going into town. His father's depression lay squarely at the feet of Henry Dean Senior. He wanted to confront him and have it out.

As expected, the funeral proved to be a sombre affair. Most of the farmers and a good number of townsfolk attended. One notable absence was that of the Dean family. Enough farmers made it clear to the Deans they would not be welcome, and Sheriff told Dean Senior he couldn't guarantee his safety if he attended.

Henry Dean Senior did the next best thing and shut his store as a mark of respect; a gesture that most folk found pointless as no one would attend the store that day anyway.

The farming community in this area were close knit, kick one and everyone limps. Unfortunately, they still had little choice but to continue trading with Dean Senior, but he soon realised it would be best if he handed over the storefront to his son. Shortly after the funeral Henry Dean Senior was only ever seen in church.

After burying his parents, Jimmy made the same vow his father made after the auction and refused to have any dealings with Dean's Emporium, despite the fact his onetime friend was now running it. Not only that, he refused to go into town at all. When the new lease for the farm was transferred to Jimmy's name, the attorney was forced to drive out to the farm to get Jimmy's signature.

The lack of social activities for Jimmy brought about a gradual change and he too began to reflect inwardly, failing to realise the change in his behaviour. His manner became more abrupt and although if questioned he would have professed his undying love for Martha, there was little outward sign this was the case.

1966

'Yes - yes, dear. I know what you said. You know Jimmy won't come, so I have done the next best thing.'

Martha rummaged in the large shopping bag she carried, pulled out a large clear bag and place it on the counter then continued poking around.

Henry stared in horror at the item on the counter. Jimmy Ellis stared back at him.

'Ah there we are.'

Martha placed a second bag containing a pair of feet next to Jimmy's head. She looked up at Henry with a smile on her face.

'See, we will get a perfect fit now.'

She frowned as Henry slowly raised his hand and pointed at the bag containing the head of Jimmy. A series of slightly muted sounds emanated from the shopkeeper.

Martha gaze travelled along his arm to the bony finger wavering in the direction of the bloody bag on the counter.

'Oh, I thought I would save us some time and me a lot of grief. He said to get him a new hat too, and to make sure it was the correct size.'

Arabian Noir

◆ ◆ ◆

The steps of Big Horn County District Courthouse thronged with people; the courtroom itself filled beyond capacity. For weeks, in bars and shops, hairdressers and gas stations, strangers and friends alike discussed the case at length, news of which spread throughout the region like wildfire. This was the biggest thing to happen around these parts since the Battle of the Little Bighorn.

The judge peered over his glasses at the defendant.

'The jury has found you guilty of murder in the first degree. As is required by the State of Montana it falls to me to pronounce sentence, but first I would like to make a few comments.'

He sipped a glass of water and referred to his notes.

'You have consistently refused to acknowledge any responsibility for this heinous act and in fact repeatedly tried to blame another party for the murder. Despite repeated requests you have continually refused to reveal the whereabouts of Mr Ellis's body therefore denying him a decent burial and you have not once shown any remorse for your acts.

'Yet despite your denials, there is overwhelming evidence of your involvement. The bloody shovel and saw found on your property, which you also deny all knowledge of and the bloody bags containing the feet and head of the deceased found in your possession.'

The judge looked up from his papers.

'Henry Dean Junior, it's ordered and judged by this court that you be sentenced to death, and you deserve death. If there ever was a reason for the death penalty to exist in this state, you're it.'

Footnote

'Thank you, Mrs Thomas. Please come again.'

Even in the hands of Mr Dean Senior, the Emporium had never done so well. Some folks put it down to the bigger premises, others to the introduction of the fast-food restaurant selling both hamburgers and southern fried chicken. But the owner knew it was more than this. New blood almost always breathes life into a new business and the chance for change had presented itself.

When Mrs Ellis flew out of Dean's Emporium that day screaming "murder, murder", the shock of seeing her husband's severed head and feet was plain for everyone to see. And when Martha Ellis took the stand in court, no one could doubt Henry's guilt. Such a sweet innocent person as Martha couldn't possibly commit such an atrocious act.

As for the motive, there wasn't a single person in Rattlebone who didn't know of his obsession for Martha Ellis. Martha knew all the right people to tell "in confidence" of his amorous approaches. The jury took a mere two hours and twenty minutes to find him guilty of the murder of Jimmy Ellis.

Over the years, Martha amassed a reasonable sum of money, so when the store came up for auction, her thriftiness paid dividends when she found she had enough saved to buy both the store and Ellis Farm. The rent from the farm helped pay for the expansion into the new store premises, and the rest, as they say, is history.

Martha never forgave Henry Junior for his actions all those years ago, nor for his family destroying Jimmy.

Hell hath no fury like a woman scorned.

AUTHOR BIOGRAPHY

Glen R Stansfield likes to kill people – in stories – mostly! He has self-published two novels, *Fishing for Stones* and *Harry*. A third, *Out of Darkness* is scheduled for release early 2024. Contributions to several print and online publications led to the release of a cookbook *Around the World in Eighty Dishes*. Now residing in Panama with his wife Jess, Glen is currently an ambassador for the Alliance of Independent Authors, encouraging authors worldwide. You can connect with him at: www.glenrstansfield.com

Jack and the Box

by S.G. Parker

◆◆◆◆

1968

Jack shook his head and refocused on his playing cards. Drunken men crowded the Bedouin tent where the atmosphere was thick with body odour and the aroma of *oudh*. Jack's crew stood behind him, jeering at the locals and roaring with laughter. Nasir, a middle-aged Qatari, stared at the money in the centre of the table, a cool £900, after Jack had gone all-in. The other three players had already folded.

Jack met Nasir's eyes and grinned. 'Your call.'

Nasir pulled a pouch from his *thobe* and fished out a bundle of local banknotes.

'Hey!' Jack said. 'Sterling only.'

'No more sterling. Only riyals.'

'We agreed the rules. If you can't match the bet, you fold.'

Nasir spoke to his compatriots, who each demurred. The frustration on his face was plain, a feeling Jack knew all too well: the torment of a gambler denied an easy win by a simple lack of funds. Nasir's eye twitched, and he beckoned over a skinny boy and

Arabian Noir

whispered in his ear. The boy recoiled, shaking his head, but Nasir barked and sent him away.

'What's the hold-up?' Jack said.

Nasir gestured for him to wait.

Jack lit a cigarette. He sucked in the smoke and took another mouthful of grappa.

A hush fell over the tent as the boy reappeared, bearing a pearl-inlaid box. Nasir raised the lid and presented the contents: a gold-clasped pearl necklace, lying on white silk cloth.

Jack's cabin mate, Bill, gave a long whistle.

Nasir snapped the box shut and slid it into the middle, creating consternation amongst the other Arab men. Jack glanced at the boy, who stared at the box with anguish. Jack nodded, accepting the bet, and again the tent fell silent.

Jack showed his hand: four of a kind.

He would never forget the expression on Nasir's face. Despite the grappa and the elation of victory, it was a look that would haunt him for years afterwards, tainting his enjoyment whenever he won and another man lost. He would imagine rewinding history and magnanimously returning the box to his vanquished opponent. He would even wish he'd folded—or at least not second-dealt himself the four jacks that won him the hand—but mostly, he would regret having played the stupid game at all. He and the boys should have taken the cash for the smuggled alcohol and got on their way. But back then, Jack had never been able to resist the lure of a card game—especially one so unfairly stacked in his favour.

So, without the benefit of hindsight, he'd grabbed the box and a handful of cash as the fists began to fly. They'd been a good lot, his crew, ready to defend the rights of an illegal gambler to the last. He'd barely made it out of the tent before the red and blue lights arrived, the police having been alerted by some sharp-eyed soldier at the nearby fort. As the mayhem grew, he and Bill squeezed through the stockade and took off into the scrubland towards the beach, half-laughing at the thrill of it, half-dreading getting caught.

They'd not gone far before Bill was tackled by a policeman. As the two tussled, Jack ran on – it was every man for himself by this point, they all knew that. Jack fled with that box clutched to his chest like it was life itself. But when he snatched a glance over his shoulder, he ran straight into a wall.

He came to, with the waxing crescent moon grinning down at him, blood trickling from a throbbing wound on his brow. At the stockade, the police lights still flashed, but the shouting had died down. Off to his left, two flashlights wobbled, his pursuers having missed his prone figure as they'd passed. He retrieved the box and clambered over the crumbling stone wall.

The ground on the other side was looser and rose and fell with an odd regularity. His feet sank into the wind-blown sand and skittered on the stone-covered hillocks. The roar of the waves grew louder. A little further and he'd be free and clear. His boot caught on a low wall hidden by a clump of grass. He landed with a crash. Scrambling to his feet, he swore as pain shot up from his right ankle.

A shout arose from 100 yards away. Flashlights swept in his direction.

He cursed. They wouldn't steal what was his. He'd won it—maybe not fair and square—but he'd won it all the same. He dropped to his knees and dug out a hole, piling in the box and the handful of cash. After marking the spot with three stacked stones, he took off at a hobble, determined to put so much distance between him and that hole that they'd never find it. Sobered by the risk of capture, he made good progress. Yet the footsteps behind grew closer, and the cautionary shouts grew louder.

At the beach, he stopped running and raised his hands, chest heaving, ankle throbbing. He gazed up at the crescent moon, hanging over the roaring waves. No need to worry. That pearl box was safe and sound. The police might give him a bollocking, but the ship's agent would straighten things out. Then, before the ship sailed, Jack would be back. He'd be back to claim what was his.

2023

On the deck of the cruise ship, Jack took a long drag on his cigarette and gazed up at the waning crescent moon hanging over the dark waters of the Arabian Gulf. In the distance, the Doha skyline glowed purple, orange, and blue, its profile familiar from the television but unrecognisable as the sleepy town he'd visited 55 years ago.

Despite having vowed to return that night, this would be his first time back. In the melee of the police raid, some bloke with an important uncle had cracked his head, creating a right royal stink, and requiring the British representative to pay a visit. Jack and his crew had been detained for two weeks until it was all sorted. The ship's owners paid a hefty fine – duly docked from the crew's wages – and the police ensured the disgraced seamen sailed straight out to sea. Jack had hoped to return on a different gig, but three months later he'd met Steph and his days in the merchant navy were numbered.

Not that Jack hadn't wondered about that pearl box over the years. Once, he'd even suggested to Steph they take a trip out here, but she'd laughed it off as a pointless extravagance.

Group laughter came from inside the ship. Jack flicked the cigarette butt overboard and walked through the light from the windows of a social lounge, where a compere crowed to a crowded room.

Steph had done that a lot during their marriage, shot down his ideas and tempered his ambitions. He'd given up not only the sea and his career but the cards, the dogs, and the horses, too. He hadn't bought shares during privatisation and had abandoned his plan to re-mortgage the house. He'd argued – God, he'd argued – but she'd refused to open her eyes to see the opportunities life offered, if only you were willing to take a chance. Instead, she'd told him she was his anchor, saving him from scuppering himself on the rocks. Eventually, he'd folded. He'd remained at the warehouse, working day in and day out for forty years. When he'd retired, the director had called him an institution.

But it hadn't been easy. The dullness of his life had left him desperate at times. Steph's attitude had also infected the children. 'I've got three kids, not two,' she'd say, 'and Jack's the hardest work of them all.' He knew that was how Jenny and Michael still saw him. He saw their looks whenever he had a bright idea. They might love their dad, but they didn't respect him; Steph was their role model, not him. Just look at their careers. Michael was in insurance and Jenny in payroll. Their idea of adventure was a long weekend in Guildford. He'd failed them. He should have encouraged them to follow their dreams, to take risks, to explore what life had to offer. Instead, he'd let Steph stifle them with her pessimism. Admittedly, sometimes she'd been right. Not all risks were worth it, and not all bets paid off. Nothing in life was certain. That's what made it worth living.

He breathed in the salty air. But he was glad to be back at sea, even if it wasn't the trip he'd dreamed of taking with Steph. A couple passed him from the opposite direction, walking arm-in-arm. He found an empty bench and plucked out another cigarette.

Steph would have enjoyed the cruise life. It was a far cry from his days in the navy—and not all for the better. Everything was too predictable. The crew must have sailed this same route ten times before, while most passengers were cruise ship regulars, who knew the routines in their sleep. Yes, Steph would have loved it.

If she'd been here.

Restless, he stood up and walked sternward.

Steph had been stolen away by breast cancer twelve months ago. The first few weeks had been the worst, back when he'd been unable to shake the feeling, she was still alive in the hospital and wondering why he hadn't gone to visit. He'd imagine her sense of betrayal and take a stiff drink. Before long, he'd be on the phone to Jenny, confessing his flaws and his failures.

Thankfully, that was over. Now he was able to see things clearly. God knew he'd loved her, and she'd given him two smashing kids, but the truth was, when you considered everything objectively, she'd held him back. If she'd relented just once and supported his plans, they could have been living the high life. She might have still been here, too – they could have gone private and not been stuck on that waiting list for months to see a consultant. If only she'd listened. If only she'd believed in him, everything would have been so much better.

He'd watched the World Cup match between Saudi and Argentina at her hospital bedside with the sound turned down – she'd never liked the football. But at half-time her eyes had lit up at the segments on local culture. He'd grinned. 'Maybe we can take a trip there next summer.' It was a familiar quip he'd used whenever Steph had expressed an interest in somewhere foreign. He would say that line, and she would roll her eyes. They'd chuckle, knowing it would never happen, even if they could have afforded it. This time, though, Steph gave only a sad smile and squeezed his hand. In that instant, the reality of what was coming had struck him head on. He'd swallowed his tears because she'd needed him to be strong, and he'd gripped her hand and stared blindly at the TV.

Jack leaned on the railing, gazing down through glassy eyes at the churning water. How could his grief still feel so raw? He drew in deep breaths and tried to compose himself.

After she'd gone, he couldn't bear to watch the other matches. He'd avoided all mention of the competition. Yet nine months later, a tourism advert appeared on TV, and he spotted the fort—the same one he'd seen way back when. For the first time since Steph's death, he'd felt a flicker of possibility, rather than black emptiness. A quick online search, and he'd found it: Al Zubarah. The fort was still there. Did that mean the pearl box was, too?

For weeks, the idea of the box haunted him until, with the anniversary of Steph's passing fast approaching, he'd signed the equity release forms and booked the cruise – 22 days from London to Doha.

Michael was livid. 'How could you not consult us? Dad, you're not thinking straight.'

The cheeky sod. It wasn't as if Jack had blown it all on a horse.

What Michael didn't understand was that this was an investment in all of their futures. Yes, it was a long-shot – the box might have already been found. But what if it hadn't? What if it was still there? Natural Arabian pearls – he'd looked up the prices – they were worth a fortune.

And it wasn't just about the money. If this gamble paid off, Jack could prove to them that sometimes in life you had to take a chance. Michael and Jenny might finally realise that if he'd only been given a little free rein, their lives would have been so much better.

A door burst open, and a group of middle-aged passengers stumbled out, ruddy-faced and cackling with laughter.

Jack turned away and stared across the water, his eyes fixed on the distant lights of their destination.

The next afternoon, Jack found himself in the front seat of a gold Land Cruiser on a sightseeing tour to Al Zubarah. Three other cruise passengers sat in the rear, all of a similar age to himself. The most vocal of them was Mona, an imposing woman with a wicked sense of humour. Her husband, Trevor, was a sliver of a man with a sardonic wit. Beside them sat Val, who was short and wiry. Jack had once spotted her on deck wearing a haunted expression and later seen her roaring with laughter with Mona and Trevor. They'd each spoken to Jack in the past, but he'd resisted their invitations to join their group. The driver was Mahmoud, a middle-aged Qatari, who wore a pristine white *thobe* and *ghutra*, and had a pleasant and easy manner.

As they exited the port, Val tapped Jack's shoulder. 'This is a surprise. You've barely set foot off the ship until now.'

'I'm not too keen on tours, but as we're flying home tomorrow, I thought I'd give it a try.'

They headed north, leaving behind the gleaming towers and shopping malls for a flat landscape of farms and pylons. When they arrived, the fort seemed smaller than Jack remembered. It had the look of a sandcastle, small and squat, with four crenelated towers. Inside, Jack scaled a tower and scanned the sun-baked landscape, trying to picture where the stockade had stood.

'Good God,' Val said as she joined him. 'Imagine being stationed here in the summer.'

'It must have been brutal, all right.'

'A lovely view of the sea, though,' she said.

He smiled and followed her back downstairs. They all boarded a minibus and trundled down a dirt road towards an abandoned town, stopping for an ageing security guard to unlock the gate.

Mahmoud led them along a boardwalk. 'This town dates to 1766. For fifty years, it was amongst the richest settlements in the entire Gulf and was home to 6,000 people.' He pointed out the perimeter walls, and Jack felt a stir of recognition. 'But its wealth made it a target, not only from pirates but also from its neighbours. Twice it was destroyed and resettled before a British attack caused its abandonment.'

The undulating landscape had hillocks covered with scattered stones and dips filled with wind-blown sand. This was the place – it had to be.

'Sand covered the town for a hundred years,' Mahmoud continued, 'then archaeologists began the slow process of uncovering its treasures. So far, only a fraction of its secrets have been discovered.'

Had his pearl box been discovered, Jack wondered? Or was that still out there, waiting for him? 'Can we leave the boardwalk and explore for ourselves?'

'Until recently, yes. Now, visitors must remain on the boardwalk.'

Silently, Jack cursed his luck.

Val nudged him. 'Fancy yourself as an archaeologist, do you?'

'Well, don't they say it's never too late to change careers?'

They chatted as they walked, but Jack's eyes lingered on the ruins.

Reluctantly, Jack re-boarded the bus. Could it still be out there? If so, he must have walked within only a few feet of it. If he could just get out there alone. As they passed through the gate, his eyes met those of the guard. A flicker of something crossed the old man's face. Jack blinked and looked away. They drove on, but when Jack glanced back, the guard remained standing, staring after them.

After visiting a bemusing art sculpture, they reached the beach near sunset and were led to a Bedouin-styled private cabana, with cushions around a low table. They slumped down with tired groans.

The beach was sparsely crowded. A group of young people played volleyball at the far end, while beside the shore, a mother took photos of her paddling toddler. Outside the food tent, three chefs toiled over flaming grills. After their drinks arrived, Jack stood up. 'I'm going to dip my toe in the water.'

'I'll join you,' Val said, kicking off her sandals. Mona and Trevor exchanged a glance.

They crossed the soft sand without talking. When they reached the shoreline, Jack stopped at the edge of the wet sand. Val waded straight into the foamy fingers of a lazy wave that sparkled in the golden sunlight. 'Oh, it's wonderful,' she said. 'Sorry for inviting myself along. But I do love the water.'

Jack gazed along the coast towards the abandoned settlement that was still visible despite the fading light. Once, he wouldn't have thought twice about walking that distance, but now it was too far. God, he hated being old.

'You seem deep in thought,' Val said.

'Old memories.'

'You've recently lost someone? Your wife?'

He looked at her in surprise. 'You can tell?'

She squinted out to sea. 'I lost my husband three years ago.'

'I'm sorry.'

'Me, too. How long has it been for you?'

'A year next Tuesday.'

'You're doing well. It took me eighteen months before I could face a cruise. Were you and your wife regulars?'

'No. It's my first time, but I was in the navy, so...'

She studied him and then resumed wading.

'Can I ask...' Jack said. 'Does it get easier?'

'Yes and no. A friend told me it never stops hurting, it just gets less all-consuming.'

'And that's how it is for you?'

'I'm getting there. But now and then, it hits me by surprise all over again.' She swung her foot through the water. 'This helps.'

Jack frowned.

She smiled. 'Not just the sea, I mean the sun, the sand, the company of friends. I wasted so much time being furious with my husband. After losing him, I decided I had to make the most of the time I had left. It might sound corny, but it's true.'

Mona called out that the food was ready, and Jack followed Val back to the cabana.

As the sun set, they gorged on chops, curries and salads. Jack found himself laughing at a story Mona told, and his thoughts about the box slipped from his mind. At last, belly full and bladder bursting, he went to the restroom. Afterwards, he lit a cigarette and took in the night. From the cabana, came the laughter of Mona, Trevor, and Val. The scent of *shisha* hung in the air. Somewhere, an ensemble played a traditional Arabic tune. He crossed the soft sand to the shore, and on impulse, kicked off his shoes. He smiled as the water washed over his ankles and pulled at his toes when it drew back. The waxing moon grinned down at him.

His smile faded as he recalled Steph in the hospital bed, looking so frail, a ghost of the woman she had been. Here he was, living it up as if she'd meant nothing. He blinked back tears, and his face hardened. He peered along the beach towards the abandoned town. You'll see, Steph; those pearls will pay off Michael's and Jenny's mortgages. They'll give our grandkids the start in life we never had. They'll be able to make something of their lives, without having to pinch the pennies.

A new group arrived, laughing and hooting, and the tempo of the music picked up. Jack glanced towards the cabana. If only he had transport, he could be there and back before anyone noticed. He hesitated, then pulled out his phone. 'Mahmoud? It's Jack. Listen, I dropped my wallet on the boardwalk...' He spun a tale, laying it on nice and thick, describing how his only copy of his favourite picture of Steph was tucked inside that wallet—which it was, it just wasn't his only copy—and he sighed about his early flight home tomorrow, and the trouble he'd be in if he didn't make it.

Mahmoud was silent for a long time before he agreed. Jack grinned and flicked away his cigarette.

The gate to the settlement was padlocked and the guard's hut empty.

'Like I told you,' Mahmoud said, 'at night, the only security is at the fort.'

Jack feigned distress. 'Is there no other way in? A gap in the fence or something?'

Mahmoud was silent. 'That would be illegal.'

'Only a little. What harm would it do? I'll be in and out in no time. Please, Mahmoud. I'll make it worth your while.'

Mahmoud closed his eyes for a moment and waved the offer away. He followed the road along the fence line, then pulled over and pointed. 'The fence is to keep out vehicles, not people. Walk towards the moon and you will reach the boardwalk. Be careful not to get lost.'

'Thanks, Mahmoud. I won't be long.'

Jack ducked between the widely spaced horizontal wires and set off. The night was dark and the ground uneven, but he kept the phone flashlight off in case of prying eyes from the fort.

At the perimeter wall, he checked Mahmoud's headlights were still there and clambered over. His memories of that night fifty-five years ago returned to him with a startling clarity – the fear and thrill, even the throbbing in his temple. With the wall, beach, and fort, he knew roughly where to search and so headed further west, trying to recall the distance he had run. The roar of the waves grew louder, and his breathing became more laboured.

Jack reached the broad location and searched the ground for the stack of rocks, but the darkness and his ageing eyesight made it futile. He took a chance and flicked on his flashlight, but in each place, he looked, he saw no stack of stones. He cursed out loud. This could take all night. Had someone kicked the stones over? He picked up his pace, despite the ache in his chest.

At the crest of a hillock, he stumbled and crashed to the ground. Jack lay there, panting, seething with frustration. His eyes fell upon a clump of grass illuminated by his fallen flashlight. Hidden between its stalks stood a stack of three stones.

He gave a shrill laugh and crawled over. After tossing the stones aside, he tore up the grass and clawed at the still warm sand. Buried stones and thorny branches scratched his fingers. Sweat dripped from his brow. He paused to catch his breath, his heart pounding, and set to work again. The deeper he dug, the greater his frustration grew. Surely, he hadn't buried it this deep? Had someone stacked the stones there as some sort of cruel joke? His frustration gave way to despair. He stopped, coloured spots swimming before his eyes. The box was gone.

In sudden fury, he lashed out and thumped the bottom of the hole. His fist struck something hard, just beneath the surface. Wildly, he clawed again at the sand. Fragments of old bank notes emerged beneath his fingers. He found one edge, then another, and caught the glint of pearl inlay. With a shout of triumph, he pulled the pearl box from the hole.

He hesitated before lifting the lid. Would the necklace still be there? Were the pearls as big as he'd remembered? He opened the box. The pearl necklace lay nestled in the white silk, just as it had fifty-five years ago. The pearls were huge.

A halogen flashlight dazzled his eyes.

'Jack,' Mahmoud said. 'You are lost. This is not the boardwalk, and that does not look like your wallet.'

'Mahmoud,' Jack closed the lid. 'I thought you were staying in the car?'

Mahmoud lowered the flashlight and stepped closer. 'You have been gone a long time. Losing customers in the desert is bad for business. But helping them steal from national landmarks is worse.'

'I'm not stealing. It's mine. I buried it here.'

Mahmoud raised an eyebrow.

'It was a card game, back in the Sixties. I won it fair and square, but the police showed up. I buried it here for safekeeping.'

'You won it fair and square?'

'Yes, I swear on my life. Look, I can give you money—once I sell it, that is. I'll give you a share. It works out well for both of us.'

Mahmoud rubbed his chin. 'Forgive me, but as I understand the rules of poker, secretly dealing yourself four jacks is not considered fair and square.'

Jack stared at him.

'The cards you cheated my father with, Jack.' Mahmoud seized the box. Jack did not let go. Mahmoud shoved him in the chest, and Jack fell back, coughing and wheezing.

Mahmoud put down the flashlight. He polished the box with his sleeve and glanced at Jack. 'You do not recognize me? I certainly remember you. When my father ordered me to fetch this box, I refused. 'He is cheating you', I told him. Yet he insisted, and so I obeyed.'

Jack saw it now, Mahmoud's likeness to Nasir, his opponent that night, the man whose face had haunted Jack for so many years.

'I swore I would never forget the man who stole it. You have aged, Jack, but you have not changed. Once again, you have abandoned your friends and taken something that does not belong to you.' Mahmoud opened the box and took out the pearls. He held them up, studying them for a moment. He tossed them in front of Jack. 'Did you really go through all this effort for my sister's glass necklace?'

Jack snatched up the pearls. They were as light and as smooth as glass. 'No! They were real! Everyone thought so.' He stared at Mahmoud. 'You did, too! Both you and your father. I remember the looks on your faces.'

'The box, Jack. I was upset about the box. My grandfather and I hand-carved this together. It is worth little money, but it was my most treasured possession. And now, thanks to Allah, it has been returned to me. As for my father, £900 was a lot of money back then.' He grinned. 'You know, you should have let him bet with riyals. Collectors these days pay tens of thousands of US dollars for each one of those banknotes.'

Jack's head pounded. This couldn't be happening. It was a con, some kind of ... He stared at the pearls. But of course, they were fake. Look at the size of them. Only royalty could afford a genuine pearl necklace like that. How had he been so gullible? In a flash of fury, he hurled the necklace away. Steph had been right. He'd been a fool then and he was a fool now. To think of all the money, he'd wasted on this trip. He should have known better. Tomorrow, he'd return home with his tail between his legs, and his kids would sigh and shake their heads. He'd be humiliated. He broke down, cursing his own stupidity.

'Jack,' Mahmoud said. 'You lost a bet. It is not the end of the world.'

Except it was, Jack thought, because now what use was, he to anyone? Steph was dead. The finality of that word still stunned him.

Mahmoud placed a hand on his shoulder. 'Come. Put all this behind you. I'll take you back to your friends. Enjoy the rest of your time here.'

'They're not my friends.'

Mahmoud frowned. 'They're not?'

Jack shook his head. Mahmoud helped Jack to his feet and turned to go. Jack made no move to follow. Mahmoud patted Jack's shoulder. 'Take a minute. I will wait in the car.'

Jack stood with his arms limp and watched Mahmoud walk away. He turned to face the crashing waves where the crescent moon still grinned down at him.

He considered the man he had once been and the man he was now, the wild young rogue and the docile old fool. Perhaps Steph had held him back, but perhaps she'd been right to; perhaps he'd wanted her to. He thought of their lives together. There had been highs and lows, but never once had he come close to leaving. In the end, it was she who had left. The house would be empty when he got home.

A breeze picked up, carrying on it the sound of distant music. He peered along the coast towards the barbecue compound. Had they noticed him gone yet? He thought of sitting around the table with Val, Mona and Trevor, eating, talking, and laughing. It had been the first time he had truly enjoyed himself since before Steph got sick. He thought of Val, paddling in the water, making the most of the time she had left.

He wiped his eyes. Steph was dead, and now he was on his own. He could sit and wait for the ship to go down, or he could become his own captain. In all likelihood, he'd end up scuppered on the rocks, but maybe, with a little luck, he would reach open water. After all, nothing in life was certain. That's what made it worth living.

AUTHOR BIOGRAPHY

Steve Parker was born and raised in south-east London. At the ripe old age of twenty-one, he joined the Metropolitan Police where he served for twenty years in numerous high-profile squads before being pensioned out with a serious back injury.

Finding himself with plenty of spare time and a deep desire to never work for anyone again, he turned an old screenplay into his debut book, *Their Last Words*. You can contact him at: www.mrparkerspen.com